DO OR DIE!

In the quiet, chilly, pre-dawn mist, it was hard for Dan'l to accept that men were about to die. Men he knew and soldiered with, maybe himself. And there was a good chance the death would not be sudden and merciful, but slow and grueling over a fire that cooked a man alive for hours.

Dan'l thought these things while he listened to the scolding of jays, the snorting of horses, the chink of bit rings and creak of leather as men rigged their mounts. Then even as the first glorious, roseate blush of dawn appeared in the east, came the warning Dan'l had been expecting:

"Innuns!" the sentry on the ridge called down. "Ten, twelve of 'em, down by the river!"

"Grab leather, rangers!" Dan'l ordered. "Stay in motion so's you don't make an easy bead. If your horse is hit, get your legs up quick so's you ain't pinned when it drops. And remember, one bullet, one Indian!"

The *Dan'l Boone: The Lost Wilderness Tales* series:

#1: A RIVER RUN RED
#2: ALGONQUIN MASSACRE
#3: DEATH AT SPANISH WELLS
#4: WINTER KILL
#5: APACHE REVENGE
#6: DEATH TRAIL
#7: THE LONG HUNTERS
#8: TAOS DEATH CRY

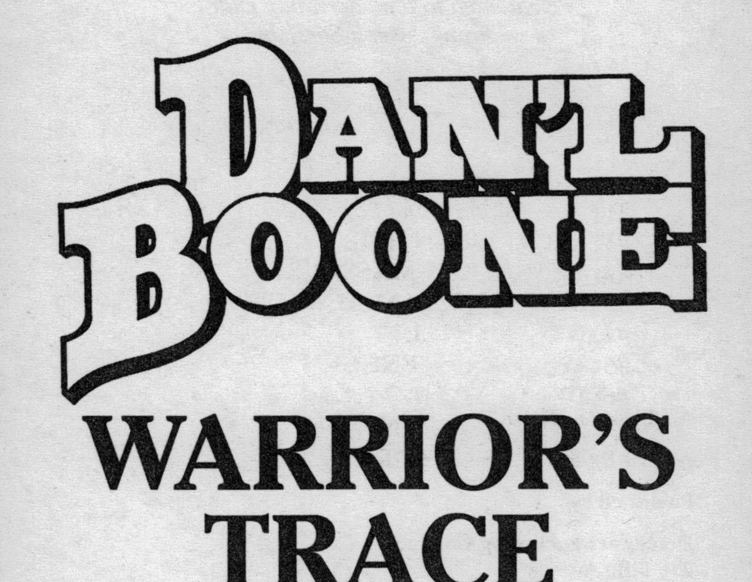

WARRIOR'S TRACE

DODGE TYLER

LEISURE BOOKS NEW YORK CITY

Dedicated to a modern-day Dan'l,
Frank Joseph Soss, Jr.

A LEISURE BOOK®

August 1998

Published by

Dorchester Publishing Co., Inc.
276 Fifth Avenue
New York, NY 10001

ISBN 0-8439-4421-8

Printed in the United States of America.

WARRIOR'S TRACE

Chapter One

After a hard and raw winter, Spring finally arrived in the Kentucky settlement of Boonesborough, as welcome as rain to dry earth.

Soon the trees were budding into leaf. Even in the high-ground hills north of the settlement, the last shadowed pockets of snow had melted to runoff. Wood thrushes and meadowlarks sent up their melodious singing, drowned out now and then by the angry chattering of jays.

Three riders dressed in fringed buckskins and knee-length moccasins emerged from a stand of magnificent silver spruce beside the Kentucky River. The lead rider sat tall on a silver-trimmed *vaquero* saddle, broad-shouldered and narrow-waisted, his body hard as sacked salt. Clear and penetrating eyes watched everything carefully from a square, weathered face. His beard was newly trimmed, but the coarse and unruly hair was thick as a wild stallion's mane.

The second rider to emerge was also a big man, but more thickset and older. Blunt and bull-necked, he had long silver hair tied off in back with a rawhide thong. He was trailed by a gangly lad of perhaps seventeen or eighteen years, a faint coating of blond fuzz covering his cheeks.

"Boone," scoffed the oldest rider, loosing a brown streamer of chewing tobacco into the new grass. "Ain't nothin' ruins truth like stretching it. And you're pulling it *mighty* thin."

Dan'l Boone tossed back his shaggy head and laughed with a powerful roar, as sassy as the first man breathed on by God.

"Webster, I swan! Thomas the Doubter didn't have nothin' over you! Hoss, I'm telling you I seen it with my own eyes, my hand to God I did! Little Jimmy Hopewell covered eighty miles in one day. On the same horse! From St. Asaph's to Harrodsburg. And he'll win this here race today, you mark my words, old campaigner."

Webster "Web" Finley sent another streamer arcing to the ground. "Pee doodles! Sheltowee, this child's been to New Orleans, you can't snow him. You figger I'll wager on Little Jim and sweeten the pot when *you* wager on Orrin Mumford. You Boones're all slicker 'n snot on a saddlehorn. But *this* hoss ain't takin' the oat bag."

Dan'l shook his head, still grinning wide. He

slewed around in his saddle to include the boy in his sly treachery.

"Corey, I reckon a man can't strike a spark where there ain't no flint. I hope you got a better think-piece on your shoulders than this here contrary pa of yours. If you wager today, put it on Little Jim and that Spanish gelding of his, Nueces. Now, Nueces is mean enough to sour dough. But that animal is a reg'lar hellcat in a race. A prideful horse, won't abide losing."

"An *ugly* horse," Web tossed in. "Only kind Dan'l Boone will ride. I figger it's like having him a looking-glass."

Corey Finley grinned right back at both of them. The lad hadn't got his full growth yet, and was too lean in the shanks. But he'd been tested during the British and Cherokee siege out west at Fort Destiny on the Arkansas River. And Dan'l figured he'd stood in for a man that time.

"I dunno, Dan'l," Corey said. "Nueces is prime horseflesh. But I got my eye fixed on that sweet little gray of Judge Henderson's. He's shy of sixteen hands, but all leg. And full of iron and leather? Well, I reckon!"

"That hoss is *some,"* Dan'l agreed. "Tough 'un, ain't he? Reg'lar war chief, got plenty of bottom. Mayhap you'll out-wager both of us, sprout."

All three men were in a holiday mood and eager to show it. Horse racing was the center of summer social life in the Kentucky settlements, and this was the first race of the new season. Not even a double wedding could bring singing to a man's blood like a good horse race.

But in spite of the pleasure looming, Dan'l

reined in his big, ugly, dish-faced roan atop a long ridge and took a look toward the west—the place where the skyline came down to meet the grass. An Indian saying surfaced from the backwaters of memory: *Courage is born in the east, trouble in the west.*

Web rode up on his right flank, Corey on his left. Both halted, shortening their reins to study their friend curiously.

"What's on the spit, Dan'l?" Web said softly, knowing that look and not liking it.

" 'Fore you and Corey come north with that flatboat skipper," Dan'l replied, "I rode out on a long scout. Followed the Kentucky to Dick's River, then cut overland to the Ohio. Scouted the Ohio alla way to the Colbert."

Dan'l used the old French name for the Mississippi.

"Saw all kind of smoke sign on the Shawnee Trail out of Spanish Missouri," he continued. "Injun runners, too, wearin' wampum beads to show it's heap big doin's. The Red Nation out west is greasing for war. Trouble is, I don't know who they're fixin' to brace."

"Ahuh." Web nodded, digging at a tick in his beard. "Innuns're mighty notional. We heard, comin' up, how the Shawnee, the Fox, and the Sauk has all up and made common cause. Happens that's so, bad cess somewheres! Ain't a one of them tribes what spits when the white man says hawk."

"That's the way of it," Dan'l agreed.

For a moment Dan'l glanced at young Corey, and an indrawn bitter look tightened the explorer's face. Back in '73, Dan'l's oldest boy had been killed by Indians at Cumberland Gap. Since then, the local threat—at least along Wilderness Road, which linked the Kentucky settlements—had been reduced by hard-won private treaties. Of course, it all hung by a hair.

And one serious source of trouble remained, completely unchecked: the vulnerable approach from the wild frontier to the west. Several tribes, driven west by settlers, had pounded vengeance poles into the ground—blood-red stakes topped by white men's scalps. Symbolic gestures that promised the red men would reclaim their land.

But abruptly, Dan'l smiled in that wide, easy, tooth-flashing way of his that made most men, and all women, like him instantly. Take it by and large, that smile said, life out here was hard. Death was as real as a man beside you, a man who never went away. It was one plague after another of smallpox or malaria, with Indian raids a constant possibility. And even when enemies didn't lurk, an unending series of natural accidents was unavoidable. For those very reasons, a man had to drink life to the lees, and live it full while God put breath in his nostrils.

"Trouble?" Dan'l said to his friends. "Course trouble is coming. When the hell *ain't* it? But we'll meet 'er when she comes and not ruin our appetites with worryin' before we have to. Gee up, Lord Dunmore!" he shouted to his homely roan, who was named after the Governor of Virginia. "We got us a race to get to!"

* * *

The race commons at Boonesborough had been established in a big, grassy dell about three miles north of the tight cluster of cabins beside the river.

Everything was already a-bustle. The nearby community of Shakers was well represented, its members dressed in neat black broadcloth suits with white linen shirts. They were doing a lively trade in their excellent flat brooms and high-quality linen goods. Dan'l watched Web send a surly glance in their direction.

"Any them sumbitches start jumpin' around palaverin' in devil tongues," Web growled, "he'll get a hobnail boot up his hinder. A man can praise the Lord without he has to jump around like a damned neck-wrung chicken."

Two grape-stake fences about twenty yards apart marked the actual running course. Spectators were scattered well back from the second fence; long, crude benches had been erected for the women and children, who'd arrived in carryalls and light Dearborns. The men and older boys, however, all crowded close to the stalls where the competing horses waited and wagering stations had been set up. It was customary to examine the contenders before wagers were placed.

Very few wagers out here, however, involved any kind of hard currency, which was scarce. Most men wagered with "bucks"—deerskins, currently valued at one dollar. Jugs and bladder bags of corn mash passed from man to man; some of the younger men made side bets on wrestling matches and ax-throwing contests—an opportunity to show off for the women on the benches.

Dan'l glanced toward the spectators, and spotted a flash of gold under a crisp white bonnet. His wife, Rebecca, waved gaily at him, and Dan'l waved back, grinning with anticipation. For Becky was sitting beside Tilly Hopewell. When *those* two had 'em a council, Dan'l knew, it meant menfolk were going to eat like conquering heroes after the race.

Dan'l, Web, and Corey found James Hopewell and his boy, Little Jim, showing off their pure black gelding, Nueces. A circle of excited male spectators crowded close to the stall.

"Why, don't be bashful, stout lads!" Big James was saying to the crowd. "Move in close, look at them fine teeth! Nueces is a four-year-old. He'll run. By the Lord Harry he'll run, or I'll eat my flap hat!"

"Why, mister, that animal is spavined!" Dan'l roared. "Got the rickets, he has. Ain't good for nothin' 'cept baiting traps!"

Several men hooted at this. James Hopewell spun around, his eyes searching trouble. But when he saw it was his friend Dan'l, the big moonfaced farmer instantly grinned ear to ear.

"Boone!" he called. "You're big enough to fight cougars with a shoe, but we'll be huggin'!"

"Ahh, I'm just wagging you, James." Dan'l turned to Long Blackford, the Hopewells' closest neighbor and the man recording wagers on a stump. "Set me down for twenty bucks on Nueces, Long."

Corey and Web had both wandered off to inspect and wager on their favorite horses and riders. Any animals marred by deep girth galls or gaping saddle sores were avoided; any mountaineer's child would tell you a spirit-broken horse lost bottom in a race.

Eventually Long's boy Evan, the timekeeper, pulled an old chronometer from his fob pocket and thumbed back the cover to verify the time. A moment later he discharged a British dueling pistol into the air—the five-minute warning. The competing horses were stripped down to the neck leather. Then they were turned loose to shake out the night kinks with some serious bucking.

"Luck to you, Little Jim!" Dan'l called out as the younger Hopewell mounted and headed toward the starting pole. "Keep his head up, he'll run full-bore."

By custom, as the race was about to begin, the men grounded their muskets and flintlock rifles and pistols on a ground cloth. It was spread out in a little copse beside the main clearing.

But as Dan'l lay down his breech-loading flintlock and eased the mule-ear hammer down, his flesh suddenly grained—feeling what his ma used to call a "truth goose." Again, as Dan'l unbuckled his heavy gunbelt with its .38-caliber flint pistol, he studied the far-off horizon to the west.

"Boone, you piker!" Web roared out, returning from the nearest wagering table. "This child bet agin ye! Your cake is dough now, Sheltowee! And if this hoss *does* lose, he means to whip you till your hair falls out, just on principle. But you watch, Orrin's Ginger will take it lock, stock, and barrel!"

"You old fool," Dan'l scoffed. "Nueces won't need but two legs for thissen."

Corey joined them, offering the two men chunks of horehound candy. All three crowded the fence just in time as Evan Blackford shot a hole in another cloud, officially starting the race.

Eight horses sprang from the gates. Right off, Justin McQuady's big bay got his off foreleg tangled with another horse, and down went the bay and Justin. But the other seven contenders were off to a lightning start.

The field flew by Dan'l and his companions, hooves thundering like war drums. Divots of soil flew far out behind them.

"*Go* it, Nueces!" Dan'l roared. "Snub his rein, Little Jim! *Snub* that son of a buck!"

"Quit crowdin' his ears, Orrin!" Web bellowed. "Tarnal blazes! He'll buck, you goldang fool!"

Dan'l felt pure awe and admiration welling inside him when Nueces pulled out ahead of the pack, heading into the last stretch. The gelding's hind quarters sank with the power and lengthening of his stride. His ears were pressed flat, the tail stretched straight out behind.

"*Lord,* that horse is a-flyin'!" Corey exclaimed.

Webster cursed a moment before Nueces should have crossed the finish. The next second, a puff of dust jumped from the black's flank, and Dan'l's jaw dropped in pure, dumbfounded astonishment. He knew what dust puffs like that usually meant.

And he was right. A flint-tipped arrow, perhaps two feet long and fletched with crow feathers, punched clean through Nueces from left flank to right. The arrow plopped to the ground in the middle of the track, glistening with something pink. The big horse crashed hard to the ground, throwing Little Jimmy Hopewell head-over-handcart. At the same time, Dan'l felt the humming *whiff* of more arrows spearing the air; they flew past him, toward the clearing where the women and children had gathered.

"Holy Jehosaphat!" Web bellowed. "Innuns!"

An eyeblink later, Dan'l's blood seemed to stop and flow backwards in his veins at the sound of a woman's piercing scream.

Chapter Two

Like everyone else, Dan'l had automatically thrown himself on the ground as soon as the ambush began. But even as he pressed flat, his hawk eyes were automatically scouring the treetops south of the track.

Those arrows, Dan'l had noticed, had come in slanting, points down. An arrow launched at ground level tended to approach its target with the nose slightly up.

"You men!" Dan'l bellowed to all who could hear him. "Look lively, boys! Could be a decoy strike! Grab your long irons and form a ring round the women and little 'uns!"

From long experience with ambushes, Dan'l knew that the first man to move was often the first to bleed. But instinct told him to go on the attack.

When he grounded his breechloader and his pistol, Dan'l had kept the curved skinning knife tucked into his right moccasin. He had it to hand even as he rose and crashed through the flimsy grape-stake fences, tearing across the race track toward the thick woods beyond.

It wasn't a wild-eyed Indian fever or thirst for vengeance that impelled Dan'l forward. He was convinced by now that this wasn't a full-fledged Indian attack. If he could nab a prisoner, the settlers might gain valuable information before it was too late. As much as Dan'l hated torture—dishing it out *or* taking it—he'd do it for the security of the settlements.

Even as he moved forward, Dan'l's penetrating gaze never left the trees. And because he looked for movement, not shape, he soon spotted them: two, no, three Indians, shinnying down out of the trees toward their waiting ponies.

One reached the ground, mounted his pony in a flying leap from the rear, and tore off like panicked game. Dan'l had time to glimpse the familiar greased topknot and tri-colored plume of a Shawnee.

The second Indian, too, would reach his mount before Dan'l could stop him. So the big frontiersman angled slightly right, planning to intercept the third before he could clear the tree.

Dan'l glimpsed the brave's broad red body stripes—made by vermilion dye—and recognized the big medicine of the Fox tribe. Foxes and Shawnees were not traditional battle allies, so far as Dan'l knew. Mayhap the rumors about them making common cause were true. Either tribe alone would be more than a handful once it had its dander up.

Dan'l charged through a bracken of tall ferns and short shrubs, hurling closer to the tree. When the brave was perhaps ten feet from the ground, he leaped from the tree and managed to land square on his horse's back. In one smooth, fluid movement, the brave yanked an obsidian knife from the beaded sheath on his sash and whipped it toward Dan'l in a powerful overhand throw.

Dan'l barely missed a stride, twisting his massive body sideways so the knife streaked past his ribs and thwacked loudly into the bole of a tree behind him. The Fox was perhaps only ten feet away now, still reining his horse around to escape. Dan'l tensed his leg muscles to leap, thinking his momentum and his vastly superior body weight should easily knock the attacker to the ground.

But the veteran backwoodsman had made one mistake in the heat of pursuit: He'd failed to make sure both of the other Indians had indeed lit out. Dan'l was on the feather edge of making his leap when he saw it from the corner of his left eye: something twirling hard and fast toward his head.

Honed reflexes made Dan'l jerk his head back just in the nick of time to avoid the deadly stone head of the tomahawk; but the solid oak, fire-hardened handle cracked into his skull like the kick of a Mexican mule. Dan'l saw a bright orange starburst, then dropped in his tracks as if he'd been poleaxed.

"It *ain't* part of no damned Indian campaign, I'm a-tellin' yous," insisted Justin McQuady, whose big bay horse had fallen at the outset of the race. "It's just one trouble-seekin' Shawnee renegade goes by the moniker of Plenty Coups. This here is 'zacly how he works. They just run his flea-bit red ass out of Lou'ville for killing hogs."

Several men had carried Dan'l to a bed of spruce boughs near the race course. Becky, her pretty face tense with worry, knelt over him to press a cool poultice on the tight knot over his left ear. When Dan'l struggled to sit up, his injured head gave him gyp.

"Mayhap that Shawnee *was* Plenty Coups," Dan'l agreed, wincing at the pain. "I didn't get a good size-up of him. But since when did that worthless renegade drunkard take up with the Fox tribe?"

"Somethin's crossways there," Web agreed. "Now, a Sauk and a Fox, that's natchral as mules and mares together. Them two is huntin' partners and has been since Christ was a corporal. But your Shawnee, he don't smoke the common pipe with no other tribe 'lessen he means to strike the warpath."

Dan'l noticed young Lonnie Papenhagen lying stretched out in the cool grass beside him. Besides the dead horse on the track, and a badly shaken Jimmy Hopewell, Lonnie was the only other casualty of the attack. An arrow had punched through the soft flesh of his inner left thigh. It wasn't serious, so far as bleeding wounds went. But Indian arrow points were often dipped in powerful toxins to cause virulent infections.

"Steady on, colt," Web told young Lonnie. "This'll hurt to beat holy hell, but ain't no way to fight shy of it. It's got to be did."

Working quick, Web pulled crumbled bark from his possibles bag and used it as tinder to build a small fire from twigs and sticks. He heated the arrow shaft until it glowed orange and, showing no mercy, poked it all the way through the wound. Lonnie hollered until it hurt so damn bad he passed out. But mercifully, Web worked fast.

"You come get in the buggy, Daniel," Becky fussed. "I'll take you home. La! That lump is still swelling."

"Don't fret yourself," Dan'l told her, placing a big, hard hand against the softness of her cheek for a moment.

"You can't kill a Boone by going for his head," Web scoffed. "Nothin' up there but bone."

"I'm a Boone, too!" Becky protested. "And these three children behind me aren't orphans, *Mister* Finley!"

"Sorry, dumplin'," Web apologized. "I meant the ugly Boones. Squire's pups."

Big James Hopewell, Long Blackford, Orrin Mumford, and some others emerged from the sentinel pines south of the track.

"No sign of Injins," James called out. "Looks like you flushed all there was, Dan'l. Them red devils just cost me the best damn horse I ever broke to leather."

But it could have been worse, Dan'l realized. He looked at Becky's worried face; the children huddled behind her, faces white as fresh linen. The rest of the women and children looked a mite peaked, too.

"Orrin!" Dan'l called. He struggled to his feet, Becky supporting him.

"Yo!"

"Pick a few men for a guard detail. Then get the women and young'ns tight-grouped and escort them back to the settlement. Rest of you men! Let's form a line and ride the woods for a piece. Make sure we ain't got red Arabs laying for us."

"Don't none of yous forget," Long Blackford reminded them, "a little set-to with Injins don't mean we ain't having our corn dance out to the mill tonight! Be good music and good victuals. Anybody wants to can stay the night."

Blackford's Mill was the last point of white civilization west of Boonesborough. A brand-new floor of split slabs had just been laid down. Now ground corn would be thrown on the new wood, and the settlers would dance on it all night long, polishing the new floor to a gloss.

Web waited until Becky and the others had begun to disperse toward their vehicles. Then he said, low in Dan'l's ear, "You thinkin' that was just that worthless red lout Plenty Coups?"

Dan'l touched his painful swelling gingerly with two fingertips. "Mighty ambitious attack for *that* drunken brave. Plenty Coups does cotton to thieving. That red son would steal the coppers from a dead man's eyes. But I ain't never knowed him to be much for blood-lettin'."

Web nodded. "Ahuh. Me 'n' you has hitched our thoughts to the same pole."

"We'll do a good scout," Dan'l decided. "Damn, but I wanted a prisoner! Well, take it by and large, Justin is right—ain't likely it's the start of new Indian wars. But we'll read the sign hereabouts. The white man's Hell ain't half full."

Until their shadows began to slant long toward the East, the men of Boonesborough combed the surrounding woods and hollers.

Dan'l was especially careful to study the area around the Kentucky River. Any concerted effort at war by Indians would mean seizure of the river. For them it was the sure, steady source of excellent game. But for the white man, the Kentucky was the key trade route to important markets like New Orleans; thus the river was the lifeblood for American settlers.

Until recently, the Kentucky had been claimed by local Indian tribes. Dan'l knew the Shawnees despised him for the land concessions he'd helped wring out of them. But Dan'l had never intended for the Shawnees to be driven out completely—that could be chalked up to trigger-happy settlers who moved in after Dan'l and decided the Indians were a plague of locusts.

But a thorough search now turned up no serious threats. The men returned to their homes, easier in their minds. Later that day, before the hills were deep in shadows, the Boones set out on the six-mile journey to Blackford's Mill.

Dan'l drove the buggy with Becky beside him and the children—Daniel Morgan, Nathan, and little Rebeccah—riding in the back. Web and Corey rode the flanks. Long Blackford's boy Evan accompanied the group. He had remained behind to spark with a pretty little red-haired gal from the settlement, Libbie Sanford.

"Boone!" Web roared. "When you fixin' to start a real family?"

Dan'l grinned and Becky flushed. Web was roweling him because Dan'l's family was notably small by frontier standards. In fact, even Squire Boone's family had been considered small—only eight children. Orrin Mumford had sixteen kids, and Judge Henderson twelve.

It was blushing Becky who spoke up. "If you'd leave him to home once in a while, Webster Finley, maybe we'd have a few more children."

"Mebbe. But if a peart woman like you can't tie him to home, ain't nothin' could. Why, all the Boone boys is fiddle-footed wandering fools. That's how's come they been to places like Detroit, claim to see them buildings three stories tall."

"Plague take you, Web!" Dan'l protested. "I did too see a building three stories tall."

"Ahuh. Shore you did." Web winked at Corey and Evan. "And two-headed Injins, too, with forked tails, ain't that right? Boone, this child won't swaller your bunk like some will."

When they weren't arguing and teasing each other, the party sang popular songs like "Hail, Columbia" and "Old Colony Times." The men took turns singing the verses, and Becky and the children joined in on the chorus. When Dan'l sang "Barbara Allen" in his fine, strong tenor, even Web had to dab a tear from his eyes.

They stopped to water about halfway, where a spring of cold, sweet water frothed up from a clutch of rocks. Despite his merrymaking, Dan'l had kept an eye out for trouble the whole way. He wasn't being cautious simply because of the attack earlier at the race commons. A man survived in the wilderness by never assuming the country was safe.

"This here is country with room to swing a cat in," Web declared as they set out again toward the mill downriver. "Why, in England a man can't draw a bead on a turkey unless he's 'poaching' on the estate of some rich toff."

"That's just what my pa says," Evan Blackford said. He was a year or two older than Corey, built more solid. "In England, he says, the rich man's always dancing while the poor man pays the fiddler."

Dan'l grinned again, for that sounded like Long Blackford, all right. Long was a stubborn and prideful man, tough as a wolverine and smart as any coon. And he had too much ambition to be content grubbing taters on some back-hill farm. Blackford's Mill ground out all the corn and buckwheat flour used in the area. And Long had plans to study law and be somebody when this area was safe for something like civilization to take root. In fact, Dan'l admitted to himself he was even a little jealous of Long. Hell of a man.

The river ran close enough to hear it purling, but thick trees and bushes kept it out of sight. They turned the shoulder of the last hill before the mill. The Blackford family lived in three big rooms on the right-hand side of the stone mill.

"Likely the Hopewells're already here," Dan'l remarked to Becky. James Hopewell's family was closest to the mill, and like kin to the Blackford family.

"That's queer," Evan remarked. "Look yonder, Dan'l Pa's old dray nag is sleeping on that bed of pine needles! I ain't never seen that old—"

Evan suddenly paled and fell silent, for he had realized only a second after Dan'l that the horse wasn't sleeping.

In an eyeblink, Dan'l switched from his usual vigilance to the hair-trigger alertness that had often saved his hide.

"Web," he said quietly, even as he tugged back the reins to halt the team. "Get beside Evan, y'unnerstan? Quick. Do what it takes, hoss, to hold him back."

Web chucked up his claybank and cut in front of the halted buggy, placing a hand on Evan's halter. "Stand off a bit, tadpole. Dan'l's ridin' in first, just to be safe."

The children, quick to read the fear in Becky's face, began to ask questions.

"Shush it, you young'ns!" Dan'l snapped, and his tone brooked no defiance. He pulled his flintlock pistol out and handed it up to Corey, who was armed only with an old German fowling piece.

"Stay with the buggy," Dan'l told the lad even as the older man glanced warily all around them. Dan'l swung down and shrugged his breechloader off his shoulder. He moved quickly, but carefully and quietly, up the slight rise to the building.

"Hallo, the mill!" he called out. A sudden, smothered shout behind him made Dan'l whirl around. He was just in time to see Web lay his muzzle alongside Evan's head—the boy had tried to bolt forward to check on his family. Web barely managed to break his fall as the boy slumped from the saddle.

Later that night, and for many nights after, Dan'l would remember that stillness just before he went inside the mill and found them. The place was almost peaceful, if you didn't look close and notice the dray horse's guts pulled out through a slit in its belly. Long had some fine-looking fox skins drying on stretchers outside the door.

He found the Hopewell children first, Little Jimmy and Seth, and the baby they'd spoiled rotten though they'd denied it, three-year-old Sarah. Dan'l felt something jump inside him, something tight and painful, and despite all he'd seen in his travels and adventures, this was hardest of all. Those children had died slow, and never would Dan'l forget the indescribable horror written on their faces.

He found the rest in the kitchen. Long Blackford lay dead with a pistol to hand, shot quick with arrows. It was easy to reconstruct. James Hopewell had been hog-tied and forced to watch while the two women were raped repeatedly, then tortured—James had literally choked himself to death trying to get free. Dan'l knew how those pagans saw it: The last thing a man saw when he died was the sight he lived with forever. So they figured they had sent this white man to Hell. And Dan'l was forced to agree with them.

Evan's brothers and sisters were scattered all over, some of them dismembered, all of them scalped. Most Indians prized a woman or child's scalp highest of all.

And then Dan'l saw something else—something bright scarlet and gold clutched in little Sarah's dead hand. He recognized it instantly—the British Cross of Gallantry, presented to Dan'l for his service during General Braddock's ill-fated campaign. Dan'l had used it to bribe an Indian guard during his escape from Detroit. Anger made Dan'l's vision go dark for a moment as he realized how the medal got there—exactly *who* must have left it there, to taunt him. To remind him.

Dan'l half walked, half staggered to the door. Web was starting to edge closer.

"Nobody comes in here," Dan'l ordered. "Nobody, damn it! Not even you, Finley. Y'unnerstan? Get back there and tie Evan up before he comes to. Web, I swear by all things holy—if he sees what's in here, he'll be ruint for life!"

Chapter Three

Dan'l's grim prediction proved sound.

The ambush at the race commons, the massacre at Blackford's Mill—these were opening strikes in a larger campaign of terror. And mainly because the settlements were still poorly organized for military actions, there was little they could do to resist. The main effort consisted of warning as many settlers as possible and then forting up at the walled settlement of Boonesborough.

Later, wampum-belt pictographs and the painted histories red men called the winter-count gave it a name: The Three Sleeps of Terror. Nothing surpassed the bloody business at the mill. But for three days and nights there were random killings and rapes in the region. Cabins were looted and burned, stock slaughtered; a keelboat loaded with valuable trade goods was burned and sunk. Going down with it were handmade saddles and shoes, fine linens, musical instruments that represented months of hard work for various artisans.

Through it all, Dan'l and Web were damn lucky to hold together a tolerable defense. Frontiersmen were hearty enough, handy with an ax and fair-to-middling shots with a squirrel piece. Some were also notorious brawlers. But as to shooting wars—surprisingly few had any military training or battle experience. Nor were such contrary men amenable to strict discipline.

Dan'l saw all this, and he resolved to fix it right damn quick.

"Boys!" roared Barry Woodyard. "There's nought to be gained by tossin' words into the wind! There's been too damned many around here—"

Woodyard's gunmetal eyes cut to Dan'l, Web, and young Corey, who stood among the rest of the men.

"Too many, I'm saying, who make palaver with savages, sign 'treaties' with 'em! I don't give a hang 'bout no damn treaties. Some say Injins is just nits. Well, mister, *nits make lice*! They may be gone now, but we're still countin' our dead. I say kill every damn red aboriginal we see until there *ain't* no more!"

"That 'ere's a cock what likes to crow from its own dunghill," Web said low in Dan'l's ear.

"Reckon the time's coming, Dan'l, you'll hafta set Woodyard back on his heels."

"That's the way of it," Dan'l agreed in his easy manner. Indeed, he'd had an eye on Woodyard for quite a spell now.

By now the common square had filled and thickened with men. This tense meeting of the Settlement Council was being held outdoors so everyone could participate.

Dan'l noticed several men had shouted support for Barry's truculent words about exterminating the red nation. Dan'l knew these men well: the group of shifty-eyed hard-tails who always seem to dog every frontier outpost.

He also knew that Barry was the lead stallion in that shiftless herd. A good-sized, hard-knit hillman out of North Carolina who put himself at the center of everything. One of those boasters just bursting at the seams to talk himself up mighty high. A know-it-all, and a trouble-seeking man by nature.

"Don't matter what tribe we kill!" Barry added. His voice boomed out like a six-pounder, the words ricocheting off the piked logs surrounding them. "If one oak bears acorns, all oaks will! Word travels quick! We can even set up a bounty on red plews, profit into the deal!"

"That hot-jawin' fool has got young Evan Blackford worked up to a pitch," Web muttered.

Dan'l had already noticed that. It was only natural that the lad would be consumed with bloodlust. But Evan was like a three-year-old colt: old enough to have strength, too young to have sense.

Barry paused to accept a jug of mash and set it on his shoulder. Damned stump-screamer, Dan'l told himself. All his big plans were naught but mental vapors.

"Now listen to me, boys!" Dan'l called out. "Sure, we're in a dirty corner. No doubt about it. Them red sons had 'em a spring dance, and they'll be back for more. But once we mate with desperation, we're gone bucks!"

"T'hell with your damn preachin', Boone!" Woodyard retorted, his voice yielding to brute anger. "Save it for the Quakers! Every mother's son knows you're an Indian lover. I can't abide a man what turns agin his own people."

Dan'l damn near laughed outright at that one. He'd "loved" more Indians onto their funeral scaffolds than Woodyard had ever seen.

"Barry, your tongue's been salted in a pickling jar," Dan'l said, his voice still easy and drawling. "Trouble is, a man can turn his tongue into a shovel and dig his own grave with it."

A long and tense silence followed Dan'l's unexpected remark. The challenge was clear as blood in new snow. Woodyard stood poker-rigid, his big-knuckled fists dangling on his thighs. The scornful twist of his mouth was habitual.

But Barry wanted no part of a direct challenge. His voice lost its bravado, but not its sneering edge. "Why should a man listen to you, Boone? True, you've cut a wide swathe or two, I'll give you that. But you've lost damn near everything you ever staked out. Lookit you! Settin' yourself up as *some,* and anybody can tell you the way of it. Every Boone in Creation is poor as Job's turkey! Why, his own woman has to take in sewin' and suchlike charwoman jobs to feed their pups while the big hound dog is off sniffin' out new lands to lose!"

It was Web who spoke next, not Dan'l.

"Boone can talk for hisself," Web said with quiet menace. "But you're a-steppin' over the line, Woodyard, when you mention Becky. Ease off that, old son, or this hoss'll air you right here!"

No one had seen it come up level. But Web's mule-ear Kentucky rifle was aimed dead center on Woodyard.

"Hell, old man! I ain't talkin' agin Becky and never have! *That* gal's right out of the top drawer. I'm just thinkin' she could've done a mite better when the Lord dealt out husbands."

Dan'l grinned so wide it hurt his face. "Now *there* you've struck a lode, Barry. But say, boys! A bunch of damned schoolgirls could be doin' this for us. I'm here to talk fightin' tactics. When it comes down to the war cry, ol' Barry here is a pup playing at being a full-growed dog. Won't be nobody tearing out of here with blood in his eye, killing any Indians he can roust out. There'll be plenty of fightin' and killin' and dyin', I'll warrant that right now. But this thing will also be done by wit and wile."

Evan Blackford spoke up. "I got no disrespect for Dan'l or the rest o' you. But all this jaw-jacking is tarnal foolishness! We got to teach them savages a lesson they ain't likely to forget!

Let's catch 'em up now before they can hide in the desert."

Several men chorused agreement. Dan'l snorted outright. Like most who had never ventured farther west than Kentucky, Evan accepted the common notion that the rest of the continent was a vast, arid wasteland.

"Colt, don't be in such a puffin' hurry. It *ain't* no damn desert in Spanish Missouri," Dan'l interjected. "And Spanish Missouri is where we got to go. Anything short of that, and we're chopping at the branches of the Indian trouble instead o' the root."

"Spanish Missouri!" shouted Lonnie Papenhagen. The youth was already limping around again after his minor injury at the race commons. "Why, Dan'l! That's beyond the Mississippi! I ain't never seen a map goes that far!"

"You think every man waits for maps?" Dan'l scoffed. "You think there ain't no history until some paper-collar writes it down? I been there, and so's Webster here. Corey, too. And that's where we got to go if this territory is ever to be safe from attacks out of the west country. There's one big trace all the red men use, and they got 'em three big caches along that trace. Weapons, food, clothing, equipment. We burn them caches, we destroy two, three years of Indian stockpiles."

"You'll *wish* it was a desert!" Web threw in. "A man can make good time in a desert. But the country twixt here and Spanish Misery is Hell pulled above ground! It's trees so close you can't get between 'em. Canebrakes so thick you'll ruin a ax blade every twenty feet. There's places where the skeeters will eat a horse *or* a man down to bone."

"Now slow it down, Dad," Woodyard cut in. "You're talkin' like it's voted and settled. We got us a settlement charter here, and—"

"I signed that charter first of every man!" Dan'l called out. "Now, I grant it's full up with fancy-fine phrases about election of officers and putting this, that, and the other to a vote. But look here, fellas! I've watched wagon companies get stranded in snow all winter on account the fools bickered and held 'elections' over who should lead 'em. Y'unnerstan' me? There's times for stump speeches, and there's times to pull your freight. This is freight-pullin' time. You with me or ain't you?"

Dan'l's tone made it clear that he was done debating. But the silent, attentive respect his words earned wasn't just the result of Dan'l's imposing physical presence. Every man there, including those who hated him, knew the facts. This was the man who'd saved Fort Destiny, ridden into the heart of Old Mexico, and known George Washington personally. The man known as Sheltowee to the Shawnees—the name they reserved for their greatest enemy, whom some even held to be unkillable. Civil to all men, servile to none. And fueled by a quiet but determined defiance of any man, or any government, that tried to keep him from yondering on God's green earth.

"Hell, you'll just get us killed, Boone!" Justin McQuady announced. "But I'm your boy! I'd follow Dan'l Boone into Hell carrying an empty musket!"

"Let's ride, Dan'l!" shouted Orrin Mumford.

This time Dan'l did laugh outright. They would be doing far more than riding. Dan'l knew, better than any man there except Web, why the word "travel" came from the word "travail."

"Now don't leave without me, boys! Remember, we got to leave more men here than can go. 'Less you boys feel easy about leaving your families to fend for themselves? It's also a good idea to wait at least one more fortnight, to avoid any late-season ice storms."

This caused such a howl of protest that Dan'l gave in with a surrendering wave. "But there's only twenty men going with me," he insisted. "No dicker on that point."

"Twenty!" young Evan exploded. "Why, Dan'l! We got three times that many!"

"Twenty," Dan'l insisted. "But twenty who'll fight like two hundred. A well-trained, well-disciplined force, each man to be tested on riding, shooting, and strength."

"Tested?" Woodyard shouted. "The hell you mean, tested?"

Dan'l's eyes cut to Web's, and both men grinned like foxes in the henhouse.

"We'll get to that right quick, Barry," Dan'l promised. "And then comes the training. Face it, boys. You've been stall-fed all winter, you've got lazy. Sleep deep tonight, fellers. Tomorrow morning at sunrise, every man who wants a crack at dyin' out west will muster right here with his horse and weapons!"

Apparently Woodyard figured he'd lost a bit too much face during the meeting. As the men filed past Dan'l, Barry spoke up. "I'll sink you, Boone. The worm will turn."

Dan'l met the man's gunmetal eyes and saw unfathomable depths of meanness and trouble. Woodyard was a bully. But not all bullies, Dan'l had learned the hard way, were cowards. One thing he did not read in those dangerous eyes was fear.

"It will for a fact," Dan'l finally replied. "But in whose guts?"

Chapter Four

"Time's pushing, lads!" Dan'l shouted even before the morning mist had burned off the common square and the surrounding hills. "You know how the wind sets around here. I'm taking twenty men on the trail. There's more than two score here say they mean to ride. Them what can cipher know that means twenty or so won't be training."

"What about Old Grandad there?" Barry Woodyard demanded, nodding toward Web. "That old man's calves are gone to grass! You spouted all that talk yestiddy about how all of us got to pull our freight, Boone. Which of us will pull the old man's?"

Dan'l felt Woodyard watching him with the steady, unblinking eyes of a rattler. His pride's smarting from yesterday, the long hunter realized. Barry had been the top dog too long without getting bit, and he didn't like it none at all now, feeling the teeth.

But Webster Finley required no help fighting his battles. And Dan'l wasn't looking for more word-baiting. Sometimes it was hard to hear what a man said because what he *was* spoke too loud. Today was a time for measuring men by action, not talk.

"Well now, Barry," Dan'l replied amiably. "That old coot *is* a mite long in the tooth, now you mention it. Son of a buck stinks, too. Don't he smell like a bear's cave? Might's well leave him behind to suck his gums."

Several men laughed and hooted at Web. Barry looked confused, then smiled sheepishly, figuring he must have made a pretty good joke. As for Web, he was so boiling mad that his eyes bulged like wet, white marbles, and the bones stood out in his face.

"A bunch of goldang *wimmin* worry about how they smell," he groused to Dan'l. Then the old trapper turned to face Woodyard.

"Barry, you're talkin' through the back of your neck! You're a white-livered mange-pot, and them runt pups you call your 'men' ain't naught but whoreson shirkers. *I'll* be tested right alongside you younger bucks. They'll make cheese outta chalk 'fore any a you little papooses whips *this* chief!"

Woodyard laughed and said, "Ahhh, save your breath to cool your porridge, you old bone-bag."

"Both of you stow it!" Dan'l barked. He shook

his head ruefully, looking at the motley group scattered around him. "Well, you wear buckskins and carry muskets. God made 'em, so let 'em pass for men! Let's get to the ridin' test, lads! Fetch your mounts and follow me."

Dan'l had the men ground their weapons for the time being, leaving one man behind as equipment guard. The day before, assisted by Corey and Lonnie Papenhagen, Dan'l and Web had laid out a riding course just north of the settlement. It wound its serpentine way for nearly a mile through dense cedar and pine forest, ending up where it started. It included jumps, pitfalls, and overhanging obstacles.

Dan'l had borrowed Evan's pocket chronometer, for timepieces were still more of a novelty than a necessity on the frontier. For most purposes, a man could gauge the time just fine by checking the slant of the shadows.

Dan'l explained that each man would be timed on how long it took him to ride the designated course. A steep hogback ridge made it near impossible to cheat by cutting through the woods.

"Every man's time will be marked down," Dan'l concluded. "I rode it yesterday noon on Lord Dunmore here, and Corey Finley marked me down at seven minutes. Now I'm timing the rest. Form a single file, boys, so we can get 'er done! You'll be sent at three-minute intervals. Web, you'll ride first."

"You ain't just a-woofin' I'll ride first!" Web hollered out, prodding his claybank up to the front of the line.

"Whoever rides behind him," one of Woodyard's toughs shouted, "best breathe through his mouth!"

Web invented some choice curses while Dan'l grinned. Only married trappers, Dan'l realized, ever learned to live with soap. Corey kept a straight face only with an effort. He had heard his old man and Dan'l lock horns plenty about Web's ripe odor.

"*Hit* it, you old goat!" Dan'l called out, and Web's horse flattened its ears, bounding forward.

Barry Woodyard moved up on his sleek black Arabian-stock gelding.

"A well-bred dog hunts by nature, Boone. And this animal was born for speed. I ain't throwing out no boast that I'll beat every rider here. That'll fall to Orrin or one of 'em. But I'll whip *your* seven minutes."

Dan'l grinned, believing otherwise. "Barry, that's as may be. For a boy raised back in the high hills, you don't know neat's-foot about horses. Look how skinny your animal's ankles are. That's a speedy horse, I'll grant, across the valley bottoms or the short-grass flats. Them long, skinny legs is good in deep snow, too. But you need a good woods pony for this course. A horse strong and thick in the ankles. Now get set to ride, Mr. Pretty Pony!"

Barry's mouth found its scornful twist. Dan'l whapped the black's rump, and Barry spurred off.

"Rest o' you men!" Dan'l yelled. "You bolted down? Close it up! This ain't Fiddler's Green!"

A few of the younger lads could barely contain their smiles; that night a few of them would be imitating Colonel Boone's colorful lexicon. But Dan'l noticed that young Evan Blackford's face never cracked into a smile. Revenge was cankering at the boy, eating at his guts—Dan'l could see that plain, and it worried him.

Dan'l waited three more minutes, then sent Justin McQuady. Seven minutes and some odd seconds after they started, Web and his claybank debouched from the thickets. Web cursed like a stable sergeant when he learned Dan'l had beat him.

"Quitcher cryin'," Dan'l scoffed. "I'll wager you beat Barry by a good two minutes."

"There's a rum customer," Web said. "Barry is one of them contrary bastards that will neither go to church nor stay home."

"Hell, you wrote the sermon on contrary bastards," Dan'l reminded his friend, though he agreed. Barry fought for the sake of fighting, and going too far to please such men was dangerous.

"But don't forget," Dan'l added, "even a bad dog is worth a bone. If Barry can't be salvaged, some of his boys might be won over. We need Injun fighters, old hoss."

Web had to nod agreement there. Hell, hadn't he been there when the trouble seeds were planted back in the '70s? The Shawnee tribe had been trouble ever since they were driven out of the huge Illinois Territory, along with Delawares, Miamis, and Ottawas. The Shawnees had never stopped avenging the burning to the ground of their huge village at Chillicothe. As for combining forces with the Fox and Sauk tribes . . . both these tribes had been off on hunts when their land was seized, villages razed, fields destroyed.

"There's plenty of Injuns needs killing," Web agreed. "But the red man has been used bad by skunks like that British dung heap Henry Hamilton, what give 'em guns and whiskey and send 'em out to slaughter the hair-faces."

Dan'l needed no such reminders—the recent scene of slaughter at Blackford's Mill still burned in his memory. But before he could comment, Barry Woodyard finally emerged on his prettified show horse. The horse was favoring its right foreleg, and Dan'l grinned slyly. The horse had probably caught that skinny ankle in a rabbit hole.

"Just a cat whisker over nine minutes," Dan'l informed Woodyard. "Old Grandad here whipped you by two minutes. So did I."

Woodyard flushed beet red. He was one of those men whose anger instantly went to his face. "So you say, Boone. Course, you held the timepiece."

"A man with a set on him," Web remarked quietly, "has the guts to call another man a liar straight out."

"Maybe he ain't 'zacly lying," Woodyard said. "Maybe he's just real careless-like. Anyhow, it don't matter. We still got shootin' and strength tests. Maybe Mr. Boone won't be able to hide my lights under a bushel next time."

Barry's hard, flat, gunmetal eyes took Dan'l's

measure one more time before the big man's horse trotted off, limping slightly.

"He's pushing a pimple into a peak," Web warned Dan'l. "You watch that 'un. You do know, don'tcha, Boone, that he was drum-headed back at the Navy yards? He knows some nasty tricks."

Dan'l nodded. Barry Woodyard had been impressed into the Continental Marines, although he'd been discharged after killing another Marine in a drunken brawl. But it was said that he'd served long enough to learn the art of boxing—learn it so well, in fact, that he'd become a military champion and a mighty-talked-about man.

Dan'l watched the timepiece and sent the next man. Then he turned to Web. "C'mon, old campaigner. Let's find out if this 'Continental Marine' shoots like us mountain renegades!"

"The hell you mean, there ain't no stationary targets?" demanded Woodyard. "That's how I learned to shoot!"

"That's how most men learn to shoot," Dan'l retorted. "And it's just about as tangle-brained as anything I ever did hear! I'll tell you right now, ain't no red man on God's green earth will give you a 'stationary target.' "

By now Woodyard was so agitated that he had to swallow hard before he could trust his voice. "Boone, some of us here ain't in no funnin' mood!"

"Nobody's playing at larks," Dan'l replied. "It's all dead serious. There'll be more training later for them as gets picked to go. But for now, you'll be tested on only one thing: your skill at snap-shooting a moving target. Just about the only shootin' you'll ever do with Indians."

But no matter how much Barry scowled and complained, Dan'l's words made perfect sense to most of the men. Dan'l had led them back for their weapons, then off again to a nearby clearing north of the settlement. Trees surrounded it on all sides.

"You'll ride in pairs!" Dan'l announced. "No slower than a canter. The right-hand man watches the trees on his right, the left-hand man watches to his left. Targets're rigged up in the treetops and controlled by rope riggings. Lonnie and Corey are working the rigs from pits in the ground. They can drop one of several targets, so you'll have to keep a red eye out!

"But you *must* shoot quick—quicker 'n scat! That's the main mile, speed. The targets will only appear for about a four-count, then they'll be tugged back up. Just as if some red son was exposing hisself to get off a quick shot. That means you don't slow your mount and you don't do no damned 'aiming.' You'll snap-shoot. Any man who scores a hit lives. Them what misses are dead 'uns!"

"First set of twos front and center!" Dan'l called out. "Web Finley and Barry Woodyard!"

"You sure that old coot can even see?" Woodyard hollered out, playing to his followers. "Hell, he might shoot *me*!"

"He just might, for a fact," Web muttered quietly.

"Hallo, target-pullers!" Dan'l shouted through cupped hands. "Stand by your ropes!"

Dan'l dismounted and buried Lord Dunmore's picket pin. Then he moved up and slapped the first two riders into motion. "Remember!" he shouted behind them. "No slower than a canter!"

"T'hell with any canter!" Web replied, urging his claybank to a gallop across the clearing. Woodyard, not to be outdone, pushed his black to a gallop despite its sore ankle.

Tree limbs on both sides rustled at about the same time as Corey and Lonnie lowered the targets—straw-stuffed buckskins the size of a small man. Dan'l watched Web move with the precision of well-oiled machinery. His musket had been resting upright on his thigh. As the left-hand target plunged down, Web threw the musket into his shoulder socket, swung the muzzle with his entire body, and blew a hole through one leg of the buckskin man.

Barry, in stark contrast, did it all wrong. When his target bounced down, the former Marine sharpshooter tried to stand up in the stirrups and shoot off-hand. It was a damn pretty move, Dan'l had to agree. Except that by the time Barry was balanced and ready to burn powder, his four seconds were up.

The target shot upward even as Barry's breechloader bucked, and he missed by a good two feet.

"Goddamnit, Boone !" he roared, reining his mount sharply about. "You had my target jerked early a-purpose!"

"Malarky!" Dan'l added with a deadpan face. "And I'm a Dutchman if a dead man didn't just call my name!"

By the end of the shooting competition, Woodyard was in a stew. His riding time had only been in the middle range, and he had failed the shooting part completely. He had an ax to grind, and he clearly meant to grind it until the wheel squeaked.

"Just the strength test left," Dan'l informed the men. "Then we break for a nooning. After you fill your bellies, the training commences for them as gets picked to ride west."

A huge section of oak log had been cut from a tree way too big to hug. It lay in a clearing close to the settlement. Dan'l lined the men up in two files.

Web gripped one end of the log, Dan'l the other. Back and shoulder muscles leaping, the two men hoisted the big log to their shoulders.

"That's all you got to do, fellers!" Dan'l called out. "You can't heft your end up, you can't go."

This time, Dan'l noticed, Barry made a point of dropping back to the end of the line.

"Barry's got sumpin' on the spit," Web muttered. "Cover your back-trail, Boone."

Dan'l and Web watched as each pair of men approached the log. Most managed to lift it, though few got it hoisted as quickly and evenly as Dan'l and Web had raised it. Corey and Lonnie, both nearly the same age and competitive as wolf pups, paired off together. For a long moment, Dan'l was afraid the determined boys were still too light of muscle—both of them struggled. But a cheer went up from the older men when they finally got the log onto their shoulders.

Evan Blackford, despite being spare of frame and small, welcomed this chance to vent his rage. He surprised big Justin McQuady by getting his end hoisted first. Finally, Barry Woodyard and Orrin Mumford moved forward. Barry made a point of using only one arm to raise the log onto his shoulder.

But Dan'l knew the big blowhard had something else up his sleeve. Sure enough, when all the men had gathered, waiting for Dan'l to dismiss them, Barry spoke out.

"Boone, folks talk you up pretty high. But a buncha damned chawbacons is easy to bamboozle. I got a better idea for a 'strength test.' I say me and you should have us a little dustup. And whoever wins will lead this fight agin the Injuns."

"Them fists o' his is poison mean," Web warned his friend.

Dan'l was a wrassler, and a fair hand with a blade, but he'd met few men who practiced the European art of fisticuffs. So it was easy for Woodyard to wade in quick and catch him off guard with a sweeping right that landed like a brick on Dan'l's jaw.

That blow swung Dan'l's head hard to the right and sent him stumbling back a pace or two. Woodyard, his big, beefy face bright red with exertion and rage, did not let up. While Dan'l was still reeling backward, the champion of the Boston Navy yards landed another solid right, a left, then another right. Each blow landed with a solid noise that made the spectators wince and gasp. But a few also gave lusty cheers of admiration.

Droplets of sweat flew from Dan'l's head with each slug, and he felt the full force of it as Woodyard swung from the heels up, all his big bulk behind the blows. After four well-aimed punches, Woodyard stepped back to let Boone drop.

But the big mountaineer, after buckling at his knees for a few seconds, shook his head and snorted like a bull. His legs straightened. Somehow, a game grin found its way onto those swelling, bleeding lips.

"Why, that was some lively and fancy work, Barry boy!" he said. "I reckon we finally found somethin' you shine at."

Woodyard was clearly surprised that Boone hadn't dropped yet. "Looks like I just took the salt out of you, Boone. *Now* I baste your bacon!"

Woodyard danced inside, easily sidestepping Dan'l's wide-arcing swing at him. He jabbed swift and fast, jarring Boone's head backward with each punch.

Again Dan'l snorted. "Well, by God, I've supped full o' that!" he proclaimed. Woodyard sneered, danced a little, waded in again. Dan'l surprised him by suddenly turning sideways and hugging him in a powerful embrace. In the same movement, he tossed Woodyard with a rolling hip-lock. The big man landed hard on his back.

He scrambled to his feet with surprising quickness, but Dan'l swept one leg out in a hook, bringing Woodyard to his tailbone hard on the ground. When Woodyard was halfway up, Dan'l caught him with a smashing right fist. The sound of it carried to the last men in the group.

No science in that blow. But Woodyard fell face-first, and only stirred for a few more moments before he blacked out.

Dan'l turned to survey the men. Already his face was lopsided with swelling, his lips so puffy he could hardly force words past them.

"Looks like *I'll* be pushing this outfit west," he announced. "Does that stick in anybody else's craw?"

"Hell, no!" Evan sang out. "But let's quit whipping on each other and give it to some Indians!"

"I'll give you plenty of Indians," Dan'l promised. "And right damn quick. But I ain't done putting you boys through your facings. Stoke your bellies, then muster back here. We'll name our twenty lucky rangers who get a chance to die hard out west!"

Chapter Five

Two full sleeps after the attacks on the hair-faces, the Shawnee battle chief named War Hawk halted his braves for their first meat camp since the attacks.

"Gliding Blade," he said, turning to a blooded warrior whom he trusted with his life. "Take two men. Move back and make a false camp. Fires, meat racks, a few stone mounds to look like figures before the fire. If the Yellow Eyes have chased us, they will make noise attacking the false camp and we will be warned."

Some tribes called white men Yellow Eyes because the first Europeans they ever saw were trappers with severe jaundice. War Hawk did not hate all white men, just as he did not hate all snakes—only the poison ones. He liked many Frenchmen, some English men, and even a few Americans. But an enemy was an enemy, and it was an honorable thing to kill an enemy. For the Shawnee, there could be no greater enemy than the poison snake called Sheltowee. When he'd taken their homeland, he'd taken their manhood, too. And no Shawnee had been more humiliated by Boone than War Hawk himself.

However, right now no one was sure of Boone's plans. The shaman named Manitou had thrown the Pointing Bone, which tells the direction of an enemy's attack. And the bone had struck a tree, splitting into four pieces! Some swore this meant Boone would attack from everywhere.

After Gliding Blade left, War Hawk returned to the fire, where two braves waited for him, the Fox chief named Iron Eyes and Scalp Cane of the Sauk tribe, battle cousins to the Fox.

Iron Eyes handed a long clay calumet to the Shawnee leader. War Hawk smoked to the Four Directions, inhaling deeply of the sweet kinnikinnick. He passed the pipe on, and as was the custom, all three leaders smoked and spoke of inconsequential matters at first. Then War Hawk set the pipe down on the ground among them, the sign that important talk could begin.

"Do you still think Sheltowee will come?" Iron Eyes asked. His broad red body stripes glinted cruelly in the swaying flames of the fire. The Fox were shorter and more solidly built than the tall, longer-limbed Shawnees and Sauks.

War Hawk nodded once. His face was handsome but cruel in the way of men who value themselves above others. The high, finely sculpted cheekbones were deeply pitted from childhood smallpox. A deep, livid scar—made by a Miami war ax—ran from just below his left ear to the right point of his jaw.

"He will come. When, no man can say for certain. Nor exactly where he will attack. That is Boone's way. His battle strategy is written on water, always his own secret. But he will come, and it will not be so long. He has found the trophy I left at the stone lodge."

The hair of the Sauk headman named Scalp Cane was still cropped ragged and short to mourn his wife and children, slaughtered by white-eyes while he was off on a hunt. He was occupied in shaping an arrow shaft from dead pine, hardening the point in the fire.

"I saw you leave that medal at the mill," he said. "And you also left a scalp you took from your sash. Are we young girls in their sewing lodge, playing coy games? Speak it or bury it! What meaning does that medal hold, War Hawk?"

As was the custom, all three braves remained impassive and kept their emotions out of their faces. Only women and white men were weak enough to reveal feeling in their faces. But War Hawk could not disguise a sudden tightening around his mouth.

"What meaning? You know that once, during the short white days, I had Boone my prisoner up in the French soldiertown called Detroit?"

The other two nodded. While he spoke, War

Hawk watched two of his men string a trotline across the nearby river. There would be fresh fish for the morning meal.

"I announced to all the area tribes that I had the king of the hair-face explorers. Chiefs, sub-chiefs, shamans, warriors with their coup feathers dragging the ground—all these arrived to view him. Only, when I raised the rawhide flap of his prison lodge, our mountain bird had flown. I found the Huron Indian guard I had trusted drunk as a Creole and clutching that medal. Boone had traded his little play-pretty for freedom!"

"That scalp," Iron Eyes remarked. "It must be the Huron's."

"You speak straight words. But raising his hair was little consolation for the humiliation and scorn I suffered that day. An Ottawa threw a woman's shawl over my shoulders, and I wore it the rest of that day, my shame was so deep."

These words shocked the other two warriors. Among red men, no insult even approached that of dressing a man in woman's clothing. War Hawk was no Indian to brook humiliation willingly. That he'd worn a shawl told them how merciless it must have been among all those taunting, mocking warriors.

"So that tells us about the bloodletting at the stone lodge," Scalp Cane said, nodding. "And the trophy whites call a medal. You mean to make sure that Boone comes for us."

War Hawk nodded. "We will not defeat him in familiar country. Boone knows that land like you know your wife's body. The westernmost white settlements are well fortified. So we must draw Boone off into the faraway lands he does not know so well."

War Hawk glanced all around them in the grainy twilight. They had camped near the juncture of the Ohio River and the great waters, which the whites called Colbert and sometimes the Mississippi. To the Shawnee, all of it had simply always been *Ouka-ulah*, The Homeland. To the whiteskins, it was the place where the Illinois, Kentucky, and Missouri territories all came together in ruggedly forested hills. Tomorrow, as Sister Sun rose from her birthplace in the east, they would ford the great waters. Then they would be in territory claimed by the Spanish descendants of the butchering pig, De Soto.

In truth, all of this area had once belonged to the Red Nation. And if the tribes could quit fighting amongst themselves, War Hawk reasoned, they could band together to get their vast territory back from the beef-eating thieves.

"Boone knows about our war trace," War Hawk said. "But he is not fool enough to try following it. He knows how heavily defended it is. That means he and his men must make their own road through land where white men have never set foot. His trail craft, they say, is formidable. But they will be vulnerable in country they have only scouted from afar. We will watch, and when our time comes, we will move."

War Hawk's eyes reflected the blood-orange flames of the fire as he looked at each man in turn. "I am indifferent to the fate of his men. We will kill as many as we must. But I want Boone captured alive. From where we sit now to the place where the sun goes down, he will find no hiding spot from my wrath! If he be in breastworks, I will drive him out! Until he is dead, we cannot hope to regain our hill country to the east. But for what he did to me in Detroit, he will die slow and hard, I swear this thing!"

"No, no, and damn it all, *no*!" Web Finley exploded in his growling, tobacco-roughened voice.

He stood, arms akimbo, glaring at his ragged squad of young fusiliers. He was so agitated that his Adam's apple bobbed up and down as he spoke. "The *front* row kneels and loads while the *back* row fires! Christ on a mule! Do you lubbers mean to blow each other's brainpans off? Why, how in Sam Hill am I spoze to make soljers outta babies? Go on back to your maw-maws and let 'em dress you in three-cornered britches!"

It was mid-afternoon, a hot day for so early in the spring. Web and his motley fighters all dripped with sweat. Training had begun in earnest, and Dan'l had assigned Web to work with the youngest volunteers.

Web was still cussing and kicking up clumps in a fit when Dan'l emerged from the woods with his group of trainees—less Barry Woodyard, who was still slumped near a water barrel.

"Boone!" Web roared out. "This hoss has 'bout reached the end of his tether! Might's well scalp each other now and be done with it. A Shawnee papoose has got more fightin' sense than these little tads!"

Corey Finley, who had been taking more abuse than anyone else, scowled at his pa. "You quit actin' like a sore-toothed bear, Pap, we'll show you how to fight!"

"Hell, you bile over like one a them brimstone preachers," Lonnie Papenhagen commented.

Web cussed some more, but Dan'l, forcing back a grin, dismounted and told the boys to stand at ease. "C'mere, hoss," he told Web, leading him aside.

"Damnit, Dan'l," Web carped. "It's bad nuff you had to pick Barry Woodyard for the list of them that's ridin' with us. That bastard will work on us like a cactus thorn under a callus. But why in tarnal hell did you pick so damn many young'ns? Hell, half them lads ain't got their growth. And skirmish? Why . . . Corey's the only one what's seen the big elephant, and he only got a peek at it."

"Now simmer down, you contrary old goat. Here's the way of it. I picked Barry on account I'd rather have trouble along with me where I can keep an eye on it. As for the youngsters, thanks to Indian attacks and the pox, we got more young and old men than we got men in their prime. We take older men, why sure, we'll have more experienced skirmishers. But how do we clear them canebrakes and trees where they're miles thick? We'll need young men to swing axes all day. Might even kill some of them."

Web calmed down a little, seeing the truth of this. Even Web admitted he couldn't swing an ax like he used to. "If youth but knew and age could do," he sighed. "Well, dinna fash yourself, Boone. I'll whip them green-antlered John-a-Dreams into men yet."

"How's Evan Blackford shapin' up?"

"Now *that* lad is hankerin' after Injun plews," Web conceded. "We don't ride quick, he'll pull stakes without us."

"Good," Dan'l said. "I need two lieutenants. You're one, and Evan will be the other."

Web looked doubtful. "A colt like him? He's sassy enough, all right. But is he old enough to be givin' orders to full-growed men like a big nabob?"

"We'll hafta try it," Dan'l decided. "Otherwise, he's got too much time to stew on things. He didn't see his folks at the mill, what they looked like and all. But he knows—he could read it in my face. That can work on a man, soften his brain. Best give him some responsibility to keep him busy."

Web nodded. He took one last look at the ragged formation, and shook his grizzled head. "Can any good thing come out of Nazareth? Lord, gird my loins!"

The training was over in two long, back-breaking, muscle-wrenching days.

"All right then!" Dan'l called out. The men, two files of ten, stood at a semblance of attention before him. Web and Evan stood at the head of their squads. "We move out tomorrow at sunup. From here on out, it's root-hog or die, boys! The days will be measured from can to can't, not by hours or the sun. Fightin' Injins is a dirty, rough, damned undignified business. And they'll be the easy part. The hard part will be gettin' to 'em!

"Gents, we've done what we can, Lord guide the rest. The main thing to remember, if you forget every damn thing else, is *never waste a shot*. We get into a scrape at night, remember that muzzle flash reveals your position—soon as you fire, roll to a new spot. And a true Injin fighter has got a name for an empty musket—it's called a war club! You don't stop fightin' just on account Patsy Plumb is spent. Once the war whoop sounds, you just start killing, and you don't stop until you're dead or the winner."

Dan'l waited a minute, letting all this sink in. Even young Evan, who so far had the look of a man who would elbow the Devil aside, stood somber, listening. Perhaps because they knew Dan'l Boone spoke straight from experience, not lore.

"All right, t'hell with chin music! We muster right here just shy of sunup tomorrow. Each man brings his long gun, his short iron if he has one, his favorite blade. He brings his ax with a spare head. He brings extry boots and moccasins. He brings powder and ball and patches. Each man will pick his best workhorse. Justin and Orrin each will bring an adze on account we'll have boats to make down the trail."

"If we're an army," Lonnie Papenhagen piped up, "what's our name?"

"Why, our hides belong to Dan'l Boone," Web growled. "I reckon that makes us Sheltowee's Rangers!"

A cheer erupted, and Dan'l grinned along with the rest.

"Aye, Sheltowee's Rangers it is," Dan'l agreed. "Until the first time you get my dander up. Then, by God, you'll be Boone's Bastards!"

Chapter Six

Dan'l had long contended that Indian attacks were way down the list of frontier dangers in the Land of Columbus. That lesson would be taught all over again at a little piece of Hell that had come to be known—without one trace of humor—as Skeeter Ridge.

If it had to happen, Dan'l was glad it would come early on and scare some sense into the greenhorns. But even before Skeeter Ridge came the first leg of the journey west: seventy miles overland from Boonesborough to Lou'ville at the end of the Wilderness Road.

"May I be *damned* if I've ever seed a finer morning than thissen here!" Web exclaimed. He pumped plenty of boisterousness into his tone deliberately, knowing it irritated the homesick men.

"May you just be damned," somebody behind them muttered. Dan'l slewed around in the saddle and watched Web grin in the early morning light, though he hid it from the men. "If Corey said that," Web muttered, "I'd whup him with a strop."

"I believe you might still whip him," Dan'l observed quietly, so the rest couldn't hear. "But this time next year, he'll come past the mark. Knock you ears-over-apple-cart."

"That boy won't live long enough to whip this hoss," Web scoffed. "Nor will you, Boone! You cross me, I'll whip you till your hair falls out, pup!"

"Ahh, I could take you, Methuselah. But it wouldn't be worth it, be like burnin' down the house to get shut of a rat. Now shut your cake-hole, old woman! Just keep your nose to the wind. You're ugly, but by God you're a coon dog when it comes to smelling out Indians."

"It's that 'ere bear grease they wear in their topknots," Web boasted. "This child'll whiff it from a mile off."

Part of Dan'l's joshing was his way of covering his own homesickness. One weakness Dan'l had never overcome was a battle in the heart—saying good-bye to those he loved. Once again, canny Becky had feigned sleep this morning—pretended not to notice when her big, wandering man bent over her with tears in his eyes and kissed her gently. And silently he had bent over each of the sleeping children, watching them for a moment before he left, perhaps never to see his family again.

But it had to be done, and his family—many families like it—was the very reason. Dan'l knew the Indians to the west had a grievance, and he'd played his part in it. But it was beyond treaties now—War Hawk had guaranteed that in blood back at Blackford's Mill. And the savages to the west would only slaughter more families like the Blackfords and Hopewells unless somebody destroyed their key supply caches along the Warrior Trace. Dan'l had observed Indians the way he'd observed game—close. Without those supplies, they could no longer support such long-distance raids.

The men were strung out behind Dan'l Indian fashion, single file with perhaps thirty-foot intervals between them. This final stretch of the Wilderness Trail, now the Wilderness Road, had been sighted through by Dan'l himself. But the Settlement Committees had insisted on log pikes, over Dan'l's objections—they caused frequent injuries to horses. So Dan'l was leading them through the mostly dense, uncleared wilds adjacent to the Wilderness Road itself.

To Dan'l, there was no such thing as safe country, no matter how familiar. So he had spent much of the time, during the four hours since they'd been on the move, scouting ahead and casting for sign. On high ridges and spines of hills, he'd spent much time just looking to get the country out ahead fixed well in his mind. After dark, those mental maps were all a man had.

They were provisioned for a noon meal, but Dan'l gave the order to eat in the saddle. Web rode up close to Dan'l and said, "The hell's bitin' at you? Dan'l, these turds got to arrive in condition to fight—*that's* the pint, Sheltowee. You aimin' to kill 'em on the way?"

"Pipe down, you jay, they'll hear you. Naw, I'll slack the pace in a few days, old campaigner. But right off, I want to keep them too busy for any extra catarumpus, you take my meaning?"

Suddenly, Web did catch on. Barry Woodyard, for starters. So far, he was too damn busy humping his weight to do much more than make a few comments that nobody seemed to care a jackstraw about. But everybody had indeed noticed the huge, ugly mouse over his right eye.

At one point, as Dan'l rode down the line of men, exchanging brief remarks with them, Lonnie Papenhagen called out, "Hey, Mr. Boone! Ain'tcha gunna remind us agin how we got to build a smudge fire when we camp on the Ohio? You ain't said it since breakfast!"

This fetched a chuckle from a few of the men, and Dan'l grinned himself. He had indeed harped on that point. But Web caught his eye, and the next grin was even wider.

"All right, I will," Dan'l said in his amiable way. "Boys, don't let it slip your minds—skeeters and bitin' flies 'long the Ohio is savage as a meat-ax! Build a smudge fire with wet wood and moss and suchlike. One smudge for each two men, with plenty of fuel to keep 'er stoked for two, three hours."

Lonnie and Corey exchanged amused glances. Of course insects could be terrible hereabouts. But to hear Colonel Boone carry on about skeeters along the Ohio, you'd think they was a tribe of Injuns! It seemed a mite queer, a man that had fought killer bears and survived Shawnee torture making such a heap of doin's over skeeters! Dan'l caught a wink or two. Winks that said, hell, every legend is puffed up a little, Dan'l Boone's included.

Dan'l had taken note of two of the best shooters among the boys: Levy Shoats and Steve Kitchens. The Rangers would be needing fresh meat throughout the campaign, for Dan'l knew only plenty of fresh meat kept men strong for clearing wilderness.

"You two," Dan'l said, cutting them out from the line of riders. "You're going to be our hunters. C'mon with me, I'll show you how to get it done easy and quick."

Dan'l led the two young soldiers about a mile through the trees until they reached a wide clearing near a salt lick. But Dan'l found only old game tracks nearby—something had made wild animals fight shy of this spot. He led the youths to the far side of the clearing.

Dan'l noticed how Levy kept forcing his horse's nose up. "Give him time to snuff the ground in strange country," Dan'l told the boy. "That'll settle a horse down quicker, once it can get the smell of a place."

At the far edge of the clearing Dan'l dismounted and hobbled his horse well back in the trees. He bade the boys do likewise.

"What's the game, Colonel Boone?" Steve demanded in a half-boy's, half-man's voice that squawked like a gull.

"Shush it, boy," Dan'l rebuked him, whipping the dust from his hat. "You ain't stopped flappin' your lips since we set out. Don't be jawin' so damn much on the trail, y'unnerstan'? Just look and listen, you'll learn most of what you need without all them damn fool questions. I ain't bein' mean, boys. I like both of you. But men who survive out here are generally word-hoarders. Now watch me, and from now on do the same. You can't be playing rovers out west in Injun country. So you got to make the game come to you if you can. Generally, you can. Most wild animals are curious, so use that."

Dan'l fell silent and took a scrap of red rag from his doeskin parfleche. He found a suitably long stick and quickly sharpened one end to a point. He tied the red rag to the other end and stuck the crude flagpole into the ground out in the open.

"Fade back into the trees," he instructed the novices. "Lay still as dead men, but make sure you got a good bead on the stick before you settle in. You don't want to be rustlin' around later."

Sure enough, it wasn't all that long before a curious doe noticed the red flapping rag and began moving cautiously across the clearing to examine this odd new thing in her closely guarded territory.

"Now with a deer," Dan'l whispered quickly, "its tail will always twitch before it looks over at you. If it looks, don't bother to hide—just don't move a'tall until it looks away again. It won't run just from seeing you, only if you move."

A few minutes later, Steve's Ferguson gun roared, and the doe bounded perhaps two steps before falling to its side, twitching in death. Dan'l quickly skinned the animal and showed the boys how to bleed and rough-gut game, butchering out only the choicest parts. He bundled them into the skin.

"Always take the gall bladder for seasoning and plenty of marrow fat to cook it in," Dan'l instructed. "If we camp for any considerable time, you should make racks and jerk some of the meat for the trail."

Both lads, jubilant after the kill, observed Dan'l's strict rule of silence on the ride back. But just before they joined the others, Steve said, "Colonel Boone? Ask you sumpin'?"

"Hell, you just did, boy! Now you got to ask two things, don'tcha?"

"Yessir. Well, it's this. Barry Woodyard says we're walkin' into a death trap. He says, well, where we're a-headin'? He says it'll be fifty red sons for ever one a us. Is he talkin' the straight?"

"Naw." Dan'l looked at both attentive youths. "Barry's miscalculated. More likely there's a hunnert red sons for each of us."

Both of Sheltowee's Rangers paled slightly. Dan'l laughed and added, "But Dan'l Boone ain't never led a man into no 'death trap' yet, and he won't start with you lads. You just quit lettin' Barry give you the fantods, hear? Do what me and Web tell you, you'll be bouncing your kids on your knee and telling 'em about the days when you rode west with Daniel Boone."

William O'Brien had brought along, with Dan'l's blessing, a gut-bag of Irish poteen. The whiskey was so strong Dan'l forbade any daytime drinking and strictly rationed nighttime indulgence. Dan'l was not a hard-drinking man himself, but strong whiskey was always useful for cleaning wounds, drawing out boils, and such.

He let the drinkers enjoy one dram when they reached the bluffs overlooking Lou'ville midway through the second day of their trek. There was a springtime balminess to the air, and the first pink peach blossoms of the new season were evident in the orchards near the river.

Their arrival, ranks closed now, caused much stirring and to-do. Lou'ville was not large, by the standards back East, but the Ohio River made it a more bustling scene than the inland settlements.

Dan'l even spotted a few wealthy men in breeches and powdered wigs. One had a black body servant. The toff turned to his servant and muttered something as they passed by. Dan'l, whose ears were as sharp as Web's nose, caught the words "swamp trash" and "ignorant bog-trotters."

Dan'l called out in his booming voice, "No, sir, you're way off the trail there! We're just hoe-men and trappers and long-hunters, trying to make our buck! Ain't one of us trots in no bogs."

"Nor pays taxes on our meat," Web threw in.

"Nor owns no damn slaves! Nor lets no Philadelphia lawyers fight our battles for us. What's your dicker, chief? Don't be whisperin' like a nancy-boy. Talk out like you own a pair!"

Considering the number of loaded muskets this group represented, the miffed citizen showed good sense in turning green and hurrying away—perhaps to count his money, Dan'l figured. Men dressed like that one had stolen most of the land Dan'l had proved up and fought for.

However, most of the Rangers, especially the young ones, had missed this scene. And now Dan'l saw why: They were casting roving eyes at a well-dressed gal on the boardwalk. She wore a pretty flowered-muslin dress, her breasts shoved way out by tight stays.

Old Web was scandalized.

"Why, they go to church dressed that away, too," he groused so the rest could hear. "Their puffy loaves pokin' right out at the preacher! Now, mister, you tell me. How's he got his mind on Jesus and the Good Book when temptation's a-knockin' on his eyeballs?"

"Satan, get behind me!" Lonnie called out.

"Yeah, cuz you're blockin' the view!" Corey added, and even Web joined in the general laughter. He winked at Dan'l. *That's my pup,* his wink said. *Ain't he a caution to screech owls?*

"There'll be no squiring the ladies!" Dan'l announced. "Close up the formation there! Look yonder, out over the bluffs!"

They did. Despite the good weather close by, they could see the onsweep of dark clouds from the north, piling up on the horizon like boulders.

"Bad storm makin' up," Dan'l said. "We got to find a good campsite west of Lou'ville on the river. We're staying there just long enough to build us a flatboat for the river part of the trip. We hump it, we can get ground sheets stretched before the rain hits us."

"As for me," Barry Woodyard piped up, "I'd give a purty sum to drink some town liquor first."

"If a pig had wings," Dan'l replied quietly, holding Woodyard's stare, "it could fly, huh? You ready to strike camp with us, Barry?"

Every man stared at Barry, holding his breath.

"Let's go," he finally muttered. "We best make tracks before that storm breaks."

But the storm held off a while, blowing east. Which was just as well, Dan'l realized. He had expected to find good timber right off. In fact, local settlers had either razed it or claimed it as their homestead, marking it. Sheltowee's Rangers ended up pushing until well after dark, riding the river bluffs in generous, silver-white moonwash.

Just before the storm finally broke, Dan'l spotted a copse of sturdy oak trees. The ridge beyond it, well within sight of the river, was high and dry. And there was plenty of good graze for their animals.

"We'll strike camp here!" he called out. "Don't forget smudge fires, one for each two men.

'Bout an hour, the skeeters will come up from the water. It rains, they'll be even thicker. Muddy up the hosses good."

Some of the men, grumbling like overworked hod carriers, complied with the order. But the men were dog-tired after a grueling fifteen-hour ride. Besides, this last stretch had been the worst. Over and over again, they'd been forced to ford and re-ford the same twisting creeks, forced to jump stone line fences, to mount and dismount continuously at washes too big to jump, too steep to ride through.

Some of the younger ones, especially, had no patience to gather fuel for smudges. They watered their horses and tethered them well back from the river, slapping mud on them as protection from mosquitoes. By the time the men tucked some grub in their bellies, topped it with potent poteen, and got their ground sheets spread, the rain had started.

As soon as the rain slacked, the more experienced men got their smudges going, heating rocks red-hot and then layering moss and damp grass on them.

"That rain'll fetch 'em tonight," Web remarked. "Corey and them are goin' to rue this night."

Dan'l nodded, his muscles already heavy. Like the men, he, too, had been "stall-fed" all winter. He had to get trail-hardened in a hurry. The hard slogging hadn't even begun.

He and Web could hear the younger men below them on the ridge, roweling each other in the manner of Colonel Boone and Old Fuss and

Feathers, their nickname for Web. No doubt they were still discussing the fight with Barry Woodyard, too.

When the mosquitoes came, they descended on the camp suddenly, like the Biblical locusts. And although Dan'l had had experience with them, they were worse tonight than he'd ever known them. One moment, there was only the lazy rhythm of frogs and crickets; the next, a menacing, steady buzzing rose up, so loud a man had to shout to be heard above it.

Every part of Dan'l's body was wrapped tight, in preparation for the onslaught. He'd rolled inside his slicker, then his blanket, and like Web, he was so close to the smudge pile he had to be careful not to catch on fire. Even so, mosquitoes half as long as a man's thumb found skin somewhere.

Web, Dan'l, and the more experienced men like Justin McQuady and Orrin Mumford knew full well what it meant when the bravado from down the ridge fell silent and the slapping noises began. None of the lads wanted to be the first to admit he was scared—not after joshing Dan'l mercilessly over "li'l ol' skeeters."

But the vicious feeding frenzy grew even more horrific, the menacing hum now so loud and steady it vibrated the very air. The slapping noises below them did not let up, nor did the urgent cursing. This was more than Dan'l had counted on, and he didn't like it any.

"By God," Web said, starting to worry about Corey. "They mean to stand pat."

Dan'l sat up, slapping at ravenous skeeters.

"Those colts gave their word to follow orders. But their word don't run no more than lip-deep. Mayhap, after tonight they'll mind a little better. They don't listen later, Webster, they'll get worse than skeeter-bit."

Reluctantly, Web nodded. "By God, them's straight words, Dan'l."

"Goddamn!"

Dan'l recognized the squawking voice of Steve Kitchens, one of the newly appointed hunters. That voice was on the brink of panic. "Goddamn! Oh God-*damn,* these sons of bitches is eatin' me alive!"

"You fools without fires!" Dan'l roared out. "Stay frosty and listen! Hie down to the river. Break you off a reed, then lay under the water and breathe through your reed."

He was going to add something else about the importance of following orders in the future, but the afflicted victims were already racing toward the water, bodies awash in their own blood.

"Damn fools," Web grumbled, even as he added moss to the smudge pile. "Might's well stay up. After the skeeters lift, we'll hafta burn the leeches off them 'warriors'!"

Chapter Seven

The next morning, only their mothers could have recognized Lonnie, Corey, Steve, and a few others, their faces were swollen so badly with bites. Most of them had ended up sleeping very little, if at all. As for Woodyard and his malcontents—they were pretty well fed up with soldiering, Dan'l could see that. So he formed all the men up just after sunrise.

"I expect a full day's work from *every* man," Dan'l informed them, keeping his eye on the sleepy lads. "And I'm also reminding you all one more time: Men get hot to kill Injuns. Then they go beat around in the berry patch and get tired of it. That's why I made you men take an oath, one you raised your hand to God for! Until this mission is complete, any man who takes French leave will be treated as a deserter!"

Woodyard made a scowl that was death-to-the-devil, but kept his tongue in his head. Dan'l looked at Steve and Levy. "Hunters, you know what to do. Get 'er done soon as you've et. Rest o'you—choose up messes, five messes of four men each. From here on out, every meal you don't take in the saddle, you take with your mess pards. I'm damned if we'll be risking twenty cooking fires.

"After you stay your bellies this morning, move your horses to fresh graze. One man will stay back to guard the camp and the animals. The others will report down at the river with their axes and whatever tools they brought. Web, Evan!"

Dan'l looked at each of his lieutenants, one beginning his manhood, one in the twilight of it.

"Each of you pick half your men for the wood-cutting detail. The other half stays for the work crew at the river."

"Now just a consarn minute here," Woodyard said. "Ain't we even going to put any of this to a vote or a discussion nor nothing?"

"No, we ain't," Dan'l replied promptly. "The settlement charter don't carry no weight out here. I'm the big nabob here, and that's the way of it. If I get killed, then you boys can have you a 'vote.' Until then, I'm the one who owns your hide. That bother anybody besides Barry?"

Nobody spoke up.

Dan'l said, "Good. I reckon we settled that real democratic-like. Any other complaints?"

"I got one," Web piped up. "You're always

banging our ears about all the noise we make. Well, mister! You snore with a racket like a boar hog in rut!"

Laughter bubbled through the ranks. Dan'l dismissed the old coot with a gesture like swiping at flies. "Now listen up. *Everybody* keep half your mind on what's around you. Remember, you left the last white settlement back at Lou'ville. I'll wager there's red men watching us right now."

The Shawnee brave named Goes Ahead was utterly fascinated by these odd hair-faced intruders.

All morning long, while Sister Sun followed her sky-road, he watched them from the northern bank of the Ohio. He was comfortable and well hidden behind a deadfall of tangled brush. As he watched, a good-sized flatboat had materialized before his very eyes.

The men below reminded him of well-organized worker ants. Half of them labored on the wooded ridge, felling trees and dragging them downhill with their horses to the rest. The other half, under the close supervision of Sheltowee himself, stripped the trees of bark and cut them into rough planks.

Each plank was laboriously notched to fit the boat's frame, then lashed into place with short sections of rope. Boone himself fashioned a crude rudder from a slab of wood, connected by leather hinges to a pole at the back of the big boat. Two men had been detailed to sail-making. Using awls and sinew thread, they sewed hides together, then rigged their square sail to a mast cut from a strong sapling.

Goes Ahead showed no impatience during the long hours. War Hawk trusted his favorite scout, and had ordered him to watch everything the white-eyes did. The Shawnee battle chief had made it clear to Goes Ahead that he wanted no surprises when Boone and his force arrived out west.

But there *would* be a surprise, Goes Ahead thought as he slid a roll of pemmican from his legging sash and gnawed off a hunk. Unless this was only the advance force, that is. Because in truth, War Hawk fully expected a large force. What could Sheltowee have in mind?

Goes Ahead's lips eased away from his strong white teeth in a scornful grin. For he had also recalled the faces of some of the youngest whites—covered with mosquito bites! Why, they were mere puling infants! Such "men" as these were coming west to fight the mighty Shawnee nation?

White men were fools—bigger fools, even, than God made them. They wrapped their feet in thick leather hides, so they could neither feel ground vibrations nor move silently. Even when standing right next to each other, they were always shouting. And talk? Whereas a red warrior welcomed silence, white men would say anything just to hear their own voices.

However . . . there was also this amazing progress with the flatboat. Goes Ahead had to admit that no Indian tribe he knew of, except perhaps the highly organized and efficient

Cherokees, could cooperate like this for laborious tasks. Put five white men in the forest, go away for a few sleeps, and when you returned, there would be a village! Complete with crops, a cistern, and a fine track for racing ponies.

Nonetheless, even the Wendigo could assume a pleasing form. The red man and the white man must remain hereditary enemies, for each group had a very different view of this world created by the Great Spirit. The red man believed that they belonged to the land; they were part of the place, like the trees and animals and rocks. The white men, in stark contrast, believed the land—and everything on it—belonged to them.

There could be no compromise between two such vastly different views. And War Hawk was right: One group must exterminate the other.

If Sheltowee could be killed—some said he could not be—that would be the beginning of the End of All for the fair-skinned intruders from the land beyond the sun's birthplace.

When Sister Sun blazed high and bright, Goes Ahead left his position. Keeping to the cover of trees, he moved quickly to the top of a tall hill well back from the river.

Carefully, Goes Ahead removed a small shard of mirror from his parfleche. Keeping it angled away from the workers on the south bank, he began flashing signals to the west.

He waited patiently, knowing the signal had to be relayed by several Indian messengers at different locations. But eventually, answering glints flashed on the horizon. Goes Ahead read them carefully. When the signal was complete, he grinned for only the second time that day.

He had not expected this order. Everyone knew that War Hawk was eager to take Sheltowee alive—to torture and humiliate him as Boone had humiliated War Hawk in Detroit.

And yet, the battle chief must have decided it was of utmost importance to stop Boone. He no doubt realized how vulnerable Boone must be while on that open boat. All this must be true, for War Hawk had given his order: Goes Ahead was to lay in wait downriver and try his best to kill Boone.

"Well, she ain't the *Mandan Queen,"* Web Finley remarked. "But by God, Dan'l, she ain't the hind tit neither! She'll float."

Dan'l nodded, proud of all the men and their good work. "She'll float. And look at that sail. Already puffed out with a favoring wind. This keeps steady, we'll make twenty miles before we anchor."

Web pulled at his chin, watching the crews man poles on either side to assist the sail. "Mebbe we shoulda took exter time to build shelters for us, too."

Dan'l shook his head. A crude shelter of planks and thatch had been constructed to protect supplies, as had a small pen in the middle of the boat for the horses.

"Naw," Dan'l said. "We'd be easier to jump at night. I want the men camped on shore and spread out after dark."

"I reckon that makes sense," Web agreed.

"Lonnie!" Dan'l called out. "Take up a pole on the starboard."

Young Lonnie Papenhagen colored like a bumpkin. "Colonel Boone? Which side is the starboard?"

Dan'l grinned while Web muttered, "Fresh from the tit, Boone. Fresh from the goldang tit."

"Hell, they ain't sailors," Dan'l reminded his friend, pointing Lonnie off to the right-hand side.

Wooded hills came down close to the river on both sides. Dan'l didn't like the way they hemmed in the flatboat. It would give a close shot to anyone hidden on the banks, he figured. But he remembered, from earlier scouts in this direction, that the banks became level and grassy about five miles farther on.

"Evan!" he shouted. Dan'l didn't like the dark, brooding look in the boy's eyes. He was thinking about his slaughtered family. But they were past help now. "Put two more men on the poles! I want good time for the next hour or so."

Dan'l's clear, penetrating eyes constantly studied the trees as the boat moved along against a gentle current. Web stayed in constant motion, his musket at sling-arms, likewise studying both banks.

At one point Dan'l caught Barry Woodyard staring at him, his face twisted with insolence. The shifty horse-trader's eyes slid away from Dan'l's.

I may have to kill that ol' boy yet, Dan'l mused. But so far, anyway, Woodyard did not seem to be stirring up his followers to rebellion.

When Dan'l estimated they were only about a mile short of the flat stretch, Orrin Mumford suddenly let out a bleat of alarm from up front.

"Sawyer ahead!" he shouted. "A big 'un. And she's a-bilin' like a pot o' soup!"

Dan'l moved quickly to the prow and shaded his eyes against the glare from the water. Perhaps two hundred yards in front of them, a huge underwater obstruction had formed, plumb in the middle of the river. The water foamed and swirled, sucking everything toward it.

Web moved up beside him. "Thissen ain't pee doodles, Dan'l," the old-timer said, worry clear in his voice. "Don't look to this hoss like there's room to squeak past 'er."

Dan'l glanced at those close, steep, densely wooded banks.

"Needs must when the Devil drives. We got to squeak past her, hoss. Ain't no room to portage around it."

Dan'l whirled and began shouting orders.

"Starboard crew! Take your poles to the port and join the others there. Pole hard toward the right bank, don't fret none about scrapin' bottom. Justin! I want you on that rudder like a cat on a rat! Hard to starboard. Orrin! You and Barry grab that sail and twist 'er to a slant so she aims right."

Every man hustled to carry out his orders. Web and Dan'l took up the two last remaining poles and worked from the prow, trying by sheer force of muscle to shoehorn their flatboat between that boiling water and the right-hand bank.

But Dan'l feared it was all too little too late—the current was quickly gaining speed and force as they were drawn ineluctably toward the sawyer. As they sped closer, Dan'l saw how big and strong it was—entire trees were caught up in it, giving it weight and, thus, even more force. We either fight shy, he realized, or we'll break up in it. And even if the men escaped, their rifles and supplies wouldn't.

"Holy Hannah!" Web exclaimed, his face going white as lard. Like Dan'l, he strained against the pole until his muscles stretched like taut ropes. He had to raise his voice to be heard above the sucking roar. "Dan'l, we ain't quite gonna clear!"

The boat was nudging some to the right, but not enough. Dan'l glanced back and saw the men's faces, looking as scared as damned souls fleeing from Hell.

"By God, we *will,*" Dan'l muttered.

He tossed his pole aside and quickly snatched up a coil of rope lying nearby. He shook out a loop and began twirling the rope, even as he desperately looked toward shore.

The river was passing through the crotch of two narrow valleys. For just a moment, out of the corner of one eye, Dan'l thought he caught a glimpse of movement up on shore. But the beleaguered frontiersman had no time to consider what it might mean.

They were so near the sawyer now that Dan'l could feel spray from it. Like Lot's wife, he had to take one last look—and his stomach turned to lead. They were less than ten yards from being sucked into the maelstrom.

"Abandon ship!" Woodyard shouted. "We ain't got a snowball's chance!"

"As you were!" Dan'l roared out. "I'll personally shoot any sonofabitch what jumps!"

There! Dan'l spotted what he was looking for—a clutch of rocks on the right shore. Praying that God would guide his throw, he tossed his loop out and snared a good-sized boulder.

"Webster! *Heave* with me, old son!"

Web, too, tossed his pole aside and leaped to the rope, joining Dan'l. A couple of men joined them. By sheer dint of muscle and will, they managed to guide their flatboat around the sawyer with barely three feet to spare.

Wild cheering broke out from the men.

"That's Dan'l Goddamn Boone!" Web shouted proudly. "The pride of Yadkin County, the hoss what opened the Wilderness Road! I taught that pup every trick he knows!"

Dan'l was on the verge of retorting when, all of a sudden, a streak in the corner of his right eye turned into white-hot pain high in his back. Dan'l staggered when the Shawnee long-arrow punched into him. Then he pitched headlong into the river, even as Web roared out to the rest to cover down, damnit, cover *down*!

Chapter Eight

As Dan'l plunged into the water, pain paralyzed his right side. He could use only his left arm and leg, which left him at a dangerous disadvantage. The water was shallow there close to shore, with very little clearance between the boat and the riverbed. If the flatboat passed over him, which it was on the brink of doing, it would crush him to paste.

"Dan'l! Dan'l, hold on, Sheltowee!"

Although Web had ordered the rest of the men to cover down from possible attack, he himself never deserted his floundering and wounded friend. Dan'l fought manfully, his face squinched small in pain as he desperately tried to hold himself up with a one-handed grip on a corner of the boat's frame.

"Dan'l! Fetch hold, boy!"

Web picked up the closest rope and flipped it out to his friend. In a tricky, risky move, Dan'l gave up his one-handed grip in order to snatch at the rope. Even as he let go of the boat, he felt himself being drawn under its weight.

Just as he was sure he was a gone coon, Dan'l felt Web give a mighty heave on the rope. Corey was the first one up, dashing forward to give his pa a hand. The two of them managed to haul Dan'l in before the boat could turn the Ohio River into his watery tomb.

Gasping for air, blood flowing from his back, Dan'l nonetheless reacted from the habit of command.

"Damnit!" he shouted, lying on his side on the deck. "You men quit gapin' at me and watch them banks!"

"Put a stopper on your gob!" Web ordered. "O'Brien!"

"Yo!"

"Front and center with that poteen, man!"

Web snapped off the arrow point in front, and quickly, before Dan'l had time to know it was coming, jerked the shaft out the back. Dan'l, no stranger to pain, nonetheless roared loudly at the fiery explosion in his back.

" 'Fraid the fun's just startin'," Web told his friend. "Mayhap that arrah was pizen-tipped, Dan boy."

Web took the jug from O'Brien and soaked a scrap of rag in the powerful whiskey. He wrapped it around the broken shaft and, never hesitating, rammed the shaft back through the hole.

The pain this time was so excruciating that Dan'l blacked out. When he came to again, the world was fuzzy around the edges and it felt like there was a knife in his back. Dan'l offered no objection when Web poured two big cups of whiskey down his gullet.

One of the men made a crude pallet out of saddle blankets, and Dan'l was carefully placed on it.

"No more trouble after you was aired out," Web said. "Should we send out scouts to go ahead on the banks?"

By now, Dan'l noticed the banks had flattened out and opened up. An ambusher could still find cover, but it would be risky.

Dan'l shook his head. "No need of it, Webster. Not for the next fifty miles or so—ain't no good ambush point."

Web nodded. He glanced toward the right bank, his old eyes narrowed in thought. "Ahuh. Besides that, that wa'n no random shot nohow."

"Naw. That shot was meant to do for Sheltowee. Special order from War Hawk himself."

Linen bandages, which had been rolled by Becky and the other women before their men left, now swathed Dan'l's back and chest.

"Good thing it went in high as it did," Web told him. "Missed all your vitals. Tore up some muscle, though. She's gon' be sore, Sheltowee. Sore as Sam Hill for a few days."

Dan'l shook his shaggy head. "I'm powerful glad you told me that, hoss. Elsewise, I might not a noticed. Now pour me out another dram of that corpse-reviver, and pour it quick!"

* * *

When the war party forded the great waters, entering the western land claimed by the Spaniards, War Hawk gave orders to make one big camp for the night.

"Should I take some men and make another false camp behind us?" Gliding Hawk asked his battle chief.

War Hawk shook his head. "No need. I have received good reports. Sheltowee is not close. Indeed, he may not even be among the living. Let all the men rest tonight. Give orders to open a gut-bag of corn beer. Tonight we will give a scalp dance."

Despite this outward show of confidence, however, War Hawk was worried. The shaman, Manitou, had advised the council of warriors to be very cautious. Manitou claimed Sheltowee was in league with the Wendigo and every other devil in the Great Spirit's creation. Sheltowee had powerful medicine, evil medicine, Manitou warned. Such talk infuriated War Hawk, for even the bravest Indian warrior would flee from a battle if he believed he was up against potent magic.

That night, before the celebration began, War Hawk smoked in a council circle with his Fox and Sauk allies, Iron Eyes and Scalp Cane.

"The mirror signals were good," he informed them. "Goes Ahead's arrow hit Boone. He was knocked into the river, but pulled out alive. However, he may not remain so for very long."

Scalp Cane nodded his raggedly cropped head. "Out here, even a minor wound can quickly become fatal. I once knew a brave"—here Scalp Cane made the cut-off sign, as one did when speaking of the departed—"who nicked himself with a hatchet. A thing so little he packed it with mud and forgot it. Three sleeps later, he died of a festering wound."

This heartened War Hawk. However, Iron Eyes did not look quite so sanguine as his comrades.

"A thing troubles me," he said. "Several times we have heard of Sheltowee being wounded. Why is it we never hear of his death? Could some of the old shamans be right? Is Boone beyond killing?"

War Hawk scowled and reached up to touch the livid scar running down one side of his face. "Does *this* look like death? Even today I still have a Cherokee lance-point buried in my leg. And twice I have been stabbed in blade fights. Am *I* 'beyond killing,' too?"

But War Hawk was not interested in discussing Boone's charmed existence. What troubled him most about the recent mirror signals was the apparent size of Boone's force.

"Had he come with a large group of soldiers," War Hawk mused, "then I would know which way the wind sets. A large group would mean an attack in force against us. Or had Boone come by himself, I would know that he meant to seek revenge against just me. But twenty men? That is a puzzling number, and this thing would be considered."

War Hawk was no white-liver. Indeed, all three of these Indian leaders had been tempered in hard battles. But in fighting a man like Boone, it was imperative to know where you stood.

Once again it was the more contemplative Iron Eyes who had a possible answer for this.

"Did you not say," he asked War Hawk, "that Boone came west on a long scout, not too long past?"

War Hawk nodded. "During the Moon When the Grass Turns Green."

Now Iron Eyes nodded too. "Is it even so? And did he discover our war trace?"

War Hawk frowned, beginning to scent a nasty truth. "No man can say that for sure. But he is a man who misses little."

"If he misses little," Iron Eyes suggested, "then he may well know about our caches."

The truth struck War Hawk like a blow. Even in the sawing flames of the fire, his face visibly paled.

Of course! The three huge caches, strategically located to support the long ride east. The three tribes had spent two entire winters stockpiling the food, weapons, and equipment without which a war party could not sustain such long trips. Indians traveled light and fast—it was their main means of survival. Perhaps they could sustain the loss of one cache. But no more.

"Iron Eyes," the Shawnee leader said slowly, "I believe you have caught truth firmly by the tail. But if you are right, and if Boone has only twenty men, then we can stop them. And what we can do, we *will* do. By the sun and the earth I live on, I swear it: We will protect those caches. Boone's clever plans are sand against the wind. And all in good time, we will find out if he is truly immortal."

"Huh!" Web grunted, hiding his grin as he watched the younger men make sure to build huge smudge fires. "I reckon they et their fill o' skeeters last night! Chalk it up as a hard lesson learnt."

Dan'l, who was feeling poorly, only nodded. "They live long enough," he said, "they'll learn a few more."

Web had used his knife to dig up and soften the ground under Dan'l's blankets. The force from Boonesborough had anchored their boat for the day. It was that indeterminate time, neither day nor night, that Squire Boone called "between dog and wolf." The poteen had been rationed out, and one of the men had broken out his concertina. Now lively singing helped some of the men ease their homesickness.

"Leastways," Web remarked, "you'll hafta sleep on your stomach. Mayhap I'll get me some sleep tonight."

Dan'l, grimacing as he changed position, said, "Hoss, your garret must be unfurnished. Now, happens I was a snorer, Becky would tell me."

"Why, hell! You ain't to home long enough for her to notice."

After an awkward silence, Dan'l muttered, "Fool, this is no fooling."

Web cleared his throat. "Beg pardon, Dan'l. I

stepped over the line with that remark. It wa'n called for—I got my family with me, you ain't."

"Lord help me," Dan'l told him. "But I reckon *you're* family, you old stinking sack of dung."

"Ahh—don't be sloppin' over." But the remark pleased Web, and he turned his face to hide a smile.

Dan'l rose slowly on one elbow and surveyed the camp. He noticed that Evan Blackford, Barry Woodyard, and a few of Woodyard's minions had their heads bent together over a dying fire. The rest listened while Woodyard spoke, gesturing often to underscore his points.

"The ass waggeth his ears," Dan'l muttered.

Web nodded. "Ahuh. Wondered when you'd notice. Seein' you almost kilt has put snow in some boots. Some o' the men is grumbling about turning back, and Barry's a-playin' on that. He knows you ain't in no condition to do much about it real soon."

"We'll turn back, all right," Dan'l said. "The minute the world grows honest."

Web nodded, starting to build up their own smudge fire. Before long the mosquitoes would appear, hungry for blood.

"Best to end it or mend it," Web agreed. "Speaking o' which—I'll go end Barry's stump speech right now. I ain't scairt o' the big Marine braggart."

"Sit still," Dan'l ordered him. "Don't poke fire with a sword."

Reluctantly, Web followed orders. "It makes me ireful, Dan'l. That damn half-face groat. Somebody needs to settle his hash."

"I already done that," Dan'l reminded his friend. "All I can do now is kill him. And I ain't sure he *needs* killing."

Both men fell silent, alone with their thoughts and the sounds around them. Steve Kitchens and Levy Shoats approached diffidently, Corey at their side arguing hotly with them.

"Colonel Boone?" Steve called from the shadows back of the fire. "You feelin' too poorly to settle a question?"

Dan'l grinned despite his pain. "The hell is it, boy? Can't a man even suffer in peace?"

"Hear that racket, Dan'l?" Corey blurted, so hot to win the bet that he forgot he was a soldier, not Sheltowee's godson. "These two chowderheads say it's wild geese in flight. I say it's a pack of wild dogs."

Dan'l had been listening to it for several minutes now. In fact, the hunters were right, though it did sound remarkably like hounds baying, too.

But Dan'l caught Web's grin across the way, and he said, "As usual, all three of you tenderfoots're way off the trail. That's gabble ratchet."

"What?" Corey said.

"Clean your ears, or cut your hair, tad!" Web said gruffly. "Gabble ratchet. T'aint geese *nor* dogs. Them's the souls of the unbaptized children, wanderin' through the air till Day of Judgment."

The two older men were not poking fun—they half believed that old back-hills legend taught them by their gran'maws.

"That true, Mr. Boone?" Steve said softly, as if afraid to profane the passage of the souls. And before Dan'l could answer, Steve added thoughtfully, "I sure hope all them little 'uns back to Blackford's Mill was baptized. Mayhap, they was among them what just flew by?"

Dan'l felt his throat suddenly pinch shut at the memory. "They'll be all right, boy," Dan'l said kindly. "Remember 'em from time to time when you speak with the gent upstairs."

The three youths returned to their smudge fires, for the insect hum was already building.

"Ahh, they're stout lads," Web told his friend. "But Dan'l, that calamity-howler Barry Woodyard is stirring up hurt."

"Look here," Woodyard told Evan Blackford and some others. "I ain't saying Boone is a milk-liver. But ask anybody back in the Carolina hills, they'll tell you—none of the Boone clan is quite right in his upper story. He don't see how he's going at this thing all wrong."

Evan listened, his lips pressed in a grim, straight line. His bitter hate for red men had grown with each hour that had passed since his family and neighbors were defiled and massacred. It cankered inside him, a tumor of malice, growing, and when it burst, he would need to express his hate in violent action.

Woodyard, watching the youth carefully, read all this in Evan's face. He chose his words accordingly.

"Boone's plan is moon-crazy, I'm saying. Crazy, on account it don't go plumb out after the Innuns. You fellas've heard it, same as me. Boone keeps a-banging our ears about how we got to 'destroy the Indian's ability to wage war.' That's a pure crock! We got to destroy the *Indian*! And that means we go back now, before it's too long a delay, and raise a sizable force. Twenty of us against the entire Shawnee, Fox, and Sauk nations? That's a fart in a hurricane."

"It is, for a fact," chimed in Woodyard's main acolyte, a part-time hide-presser and full-time drunkard named Stone Ludlow. "This here is the thing with Boone—no man is ever as big as the reputation. Boone can fight. But if he can avoid a set-to, he will. This foolish plan to destroy war caches ain't nothing but washing bricks. Like Barry is saying, avoiding a fight with redskins is like ignoring a squeaky axle—it'll only lead to bigger troubles."

Evan finally nodded. "I'm damned twice over if I care for the idea of going back. But you fellows're right. Weeds has got to be pulled by the roots, my—my pa, may he rest in peace, used to say. So what do we do?"

"The cat sits by the gopher hole," Woodyard replied. "We watch for the main chance. Then when it comes, we take it."

"You mean . . . mutiny?"

Barry Woodyard's gunmetal eyes were like chips of flint in the flickering firelight. "Remember, boy. If it prosper, none dare call it treason."

"You with us?" Ludlow demanded. "This ain't no time to be neither up the well nor down."

"I'm with you," Evan said. "But no killing of our own, is that clear? I ain't in agreement with

Dan'l and Web, but I got no disrespect for either of 'em."

Woodyard glanced briefly over at Stone, and both men looked away, struggling not to smile.

"Nobody said nothing about no killing," Woodyard assured Evan. "You just keep this little plan close to your vest and one eye out for the main chance."

Chapter Nine

The next morning, Steve and Levy returned to camp with a plump doe, already rough-gutted. The men cooked meat and mixed cornmeal with water, throwing little balls of it into the ashes to bake. Web sent a detail down close to the river to dig seep holes in the mud. The water that filled them was cleaner and sweeter. The men drank their fill and dumped any old water from their canteens, then refilled them. Then the animals were led in from their night graze to drink.

Dan'l watched as Web walked the south bank of the river in both directions, looking for sign.

"Nothin' but animals," Web reported when he returned, sounding well satisfied. "And all kinds of 'em. Coon, deer, wolf, fox, prickly beaver"—Web's word for porcupines—"even a few buff.

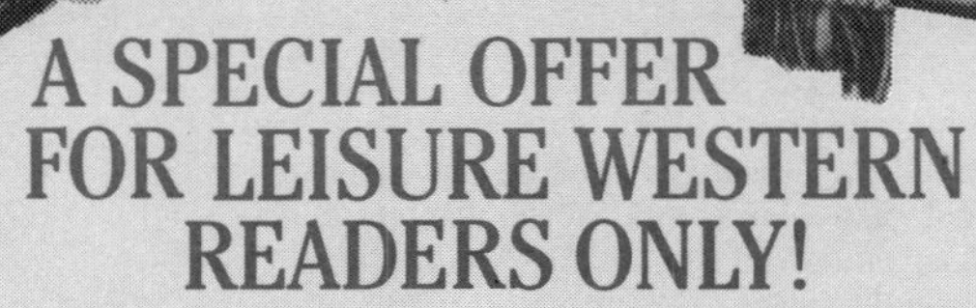

A SPECIAL OFFER FOR LEISURE WESTERN READERS ONLY!

Get FOUR FREE Western Novels

Travel to the Old West in all its glory and drama—without leaving your home!

Plus, you'll save between $3.00 and $6.00 every time you buy!

But no men, red nor white. And that's just how this hoss likes it. No Injins to raise your hair, no gum'ments to tax your meat."

"There'll be a government when we ford the Big Muddy," Dan'l assured him. "The Espanish. But I don't expect we'll see much sign of 'em. Way I hear it told, the fish-eaters've got their hands full fightin' the tribes down Old Mex way."

"Ahuh." Web spat a brown streamer of eating tobacco, watching Dan'l wince as he sat up to pull his boots on. Lonnie Papenhagen was passing by, and noticed his commander struggling.

"I'll get them for you, sir!" the youth offered, hurrying over and grabbing hold of one of Dan'l's boots. "How you feelin' this morning, Mr. Boone?"

"I'm tolerable well, boy," Dan'l grumbled, knocking his hand away. "Don't coddle me! I noticed yestiddy how the hammer of your weapon is pitted with rust. I'll feel a hell of a lot better you take care of that and let me dress myself."

"Yessir," the boy mumbled, blushing and hurrying away.

"Damn," Dan'l muttered. "He even colors up like a schoolgirl."

"Like I was sayin' 'fore that pup butted in," Web resumed, "if the Espanish was doin' their job, them redskins what hit us wouldn't have 'em a damned safe haven. There's so much room out west, why, hell! A man could never run 'em down and pen 'em."

"Strike a light! Old Rawhead Finley finally figured out what we're doing. We can't pen 'em. But we can make it too dang hard for them to get at us. Paintin' the landscape with Injun blood ain't the point. All that does is guarantee a vengeance pole and more fightin'. The point is to make sure the folks back in the settlements can go to bed nights and expect to get up come sunrise."

Web said, "You're a good talker, Boone. Pity you're so goddamn ugly. If fellers like you was goin' into politics, why, hell! I might vote now and agin. A man don't mind standin' in the rain to vote for a slick talker what can also do. Well, where is these caches?"

"Closest one is in the bluffs over the Flat River. Next one after that is near the old French Lick branch of the Missouri. The third is about forty miles beyond. It'll put us through misery to get at any of 'em. From this end, it's pure canebrake country to reach the Flat River."

Web scowled. "Them red sons is lazy bastards. *They* ain't cuttin' through no goldang canebrakes and such."

Dan'l shook his head. "They got a trace, and only they know it. I got a hunch, general-like, where it ought to be. Every path a savage uses is just a game trace he followed, lookin' to fill his belly. But I ain't looking for it, old campaigner. You know how Injuns feel about an enemy who walks their trace—we got too many youngsters along. There's a heap o' country out there, so I'm following a plumb line."

Dan'l's weathered face squinched up in pain as he tried to stretch his muscles, instantly tormenting his wounded back. "Lord, I'd give a purty price for a shuck mattress."

"Do tell? And if a pig had wings, I reckon it'd fly."

Dan'l gulped in pain as he tugged on his boot. "That's mite unspiritual of you, hoss," he said in his lazy drawl.

"Speakin' of that," Web said quietly, " 'pears to me that Evan and Barry is feedin' from the same trough."

Dan'l nodded, slowly rising. He would spend much of this day on his back. But he knew he had to walk around some to keep from going too stiff.

"I suspicioned that," he answered.

"The thing of it is, you done ruffled all Barry's feathers good when you whupped him. Now he's a-broodin'. Won't rest till you're shoveling coal in Hell."

"If he's feelin' froggy," Dan'l said easily, strapping his pistol belt on, "I reckon he'll jump. I ain't crowdin' the man."

All this was true. Yet something in Dan'l's mischievous tone made Web study his friend's face a little closer.

"God's galoshes, Boone! A sane man would look a little fidgety. Fess up! You're havin' the time of your ornery life, playing cat and mouse with ol' Barry, ain'tcher? That's why you made sure he come along! So's you could have you a little game of Aunt Sally?"

Dan'l grinned, then winked. "Me, I just chop wood and let the chips fall where they may. I ain't no trouble-seeking man, Web."

"No you ain't," Web agreed. "You don't need to be, you was born a Boone. Trouble makes a point a lookin' *you* boys up reg'lar-like."

The flatboat got under way an hour after dawn, a slight favoring wind assisting a quick spring current.

A pewter sky early on cleared to a cloudless, hot day with fitful gusts that occasionally bowed the mast. Dan'l noticed, fighting back grins, that Web was like a tomcat on the prowl, missing nothing. He made sure that Barry Woodyard worked among men who did not favor his schemes.

They encountered two more sawyers as the morning shadows began to flatten. But neither was like the whirling maelstrom of the previous day.

Dan'l got up from his saddle-blanket pallet once every hour or so, and took a wobbly turn around the deck. On one pass around, he caught Evan alone near the horse pen, filling his powder flask.

"If what happened to your people," Dan'l remarked without preamble, looking Evan straight in the eye, "happened to mine, I don't rightly know how I'd act. But I'd want justice. If you want to call that revenge, by God, call it revenge. It's true I ain't looking for no Indian war this trip west. But I do pray that the big Indian who ordered your family treated that-a-way is going to die a hard death."

Evan's dull, flat gaze suddenly quickened

with the vitality of burning hate. "You know who he is?"

"I know him, Evan. And I'll tell the world, he ain't typical of no tribe but Satan's. A prideful man, dangerous prideful. I humbled him once, humbled him bad. We've seen his answer. And now the criminal sonofabitch is marked to die."

"He's marked," Evan agreed, "with B for Blackford. I want that low-crawling pond scum, Dan'l. I want him worser 'n they thirst in Hell."

Dan'l nodded. "The Lord Jesus counsels us to walk away from it, and I love the Lord. But my pap was right, I'm thinking, when he said that now and again we need the hard God of Moses. I promise you this, trooper. I'll do everything in my power to let you serve him justice. But he's a blooded warrior with ten years fightin' experience. If I see the chance, I'm sending him under myself."

Evan wasn't exactly pleased with that arrangement. But Dan'l Boone was a man of his word, and it was at least a chance to avenge his great hate.

Dan'l glanced toward the starboard, where Barry Woodyard was assisting on the poles. Woodyard scowled as he watched Evan talk with Boone.

"But y'unnerstan, you keep a-listenin' to Barry, you'll end up on a foolish Indian-slaughter campaign. He's just lookin' to raise a ruckus, the blamed fool. You'll kill Choctaws, Cherokees, Chickasaws, whatever the hell red aboriginals cross your trail. Meantime, the Indian what ordered your people done for goes free to kill again."

"Great day in the morning!" Web roared out. "Hell'va whirly comin' up midstream! Hard right, boys! Sling your hooks, goddamnit! Hard right! Mumford, Shoats! Haul that sail!"

Dan'l limped quickly forward, pain throbbing in his wound. He could see white foam churning out ahead, marking a good-sized sawyer.

"We got room!" he declared confidently. "More poles on the port! You boys get set to duck. We can clear the bank, but we're goin' to scrape them trees."

Dan'l knew he was too unsteady on his feet. He returned to his pallet. As he predicted, the big, clumsy flatboat nonetheless cleared the sawyer by several yards. But a flexible wall of tree limbs suddenly slapped at the boat with a rough scraping sound.

Dan'l heard the first shouts even as he detected the first angry buzzing.

"Holy Hannah!" Web bellowed. "We tore into a wasp colony! *Big* sonofabitch colony!"

Dan'l threw a glance overhead and immediately spotted them—the dry, papery clusters of wasp nests, hundreds of them, being ripped and shaken and smashed as the boat caromed into the trees. The infuriated insects darkened the air like a sudden cloud of soot—deadly soot.

Even before Dan'l could get the blankets over his head, he was stung in the face and neck, several times, one stinger plunging into the tender skin of his lower lip.

Men howled with terrible pain, some getting

dozens of stings in seconds, including in their eyes and the insides of their mouths. The horses, too, whinnied in fright and pain.

Instinctively, men hit the water and started swimming away from the boat underwater. Dan'l knew, from Web's frightened cussing, that the old-timer was loosing the horses so they, too, could escape this sure death. There was no choice but to spring them and try to round them up later.

Dan'l had no time to worry about it. Nor, in his condition, could he run, leap, or swim for it. Wasps were finding their way under the blanket, making it lively for the lone man on the wildly floundering flatboat.

Trapped as he was, Dan'l could not check the progress of the boat. But it was indeed making progress—maybe too damn much. It had cleared the trees, for Dan'l no longer heard them scraping. The furious wasps deserted the ship as their victims did likewise, trying to chase them down.

Cursing, slapping at a few last stragglers that managed to get him, Dan'l crawled out from the blankets. The boat was canted at a reckless angle, traveling with the current but swirling crazily. He could see and hear the men and animals behind him, a bedlam of racket.

Staggering, twice almost going overboard, Dan'l got back to the rudder and leaned on it hard. At first the boat resisted his efforts like a stubborn ox. Then, first by inches, then by rapid feet, it began to nose around straight in the current.

Doing it gradually, Dan'l deliberately ran the boat aground on the south bank. He watched men crawl out of the river behind him and take off after the horses. For the better part of the next hour they staggered in, swollen and cussing.

It was Dan'l who laughed first. Laughed sudden and hard, so hard it hurt and made his wound bleed a little.

"The hell's so all-fired humorous?" Web demanded. The old codger's cheeks were swollen lumps above his grizzled beard.

"Hell, I like to died!" Dan'l exclaimed when he could get his breath. "Watchin' all you jaspers take off like scalded dogs! It—"

Dan'l abruptly fell silent. "Where's McQuady?" he asked.

Even as he said it, a pitiful wail sounded from about fifty yards behind them.

"Evan!" Dan'l barked. "Take two men. See him, washed up on that clutch of rocks? Move fast, fellers, them wasps might cross the river."

Soon Justin McQuady was stretched out on the grassy bank near the boat, moaning like a dying animal. When moaning wasn't enough, he screamed outright. And every man there saw why. His right arm was broken, the worst kind of break possible. The kind where shattered bone poked through the skin.

"We might set that arm," Web said low to Dan'l. "But I wouldn't put one red penny on it doin' anything 'cept to kill him. You see how filthy that wound is? That'n's past a whiskey wash! He'll be swole up with pizen come noon tomorrow."

Dan'l watched O'Brien coaxing poteen down Justin's throat between screams.

"Take the arm, Dan'l?" Web asked him.

Dan'l knew there was no other choice. Yet he was slow to nod yes. Not one man among them did not depend on his arms to make his living. Men with missing arms didn't survive out there. They sold matches on street corners back East.

"We dang well better," he finally replied. "Naught else for it. Justin's got starch in his collar, he'll take it like a man."

The two old trail friends had done this before, and watched it being done even more times. The thing of it was to just do it, quick and full-bore, and not to give anybody time to look at the meaning of it too close.

Justin needed no windy explanations. He let the men get him stone drunk, and passed in and out of awareness like a man riding through patchy fog.

"Laws, Dan'l, it hurts sumpin' fierce," he muttered when he saw Dan'l kneeling close by him. "Lop that busted wing off, Sheltowee, and throw the sonofabitch in the river. I don't ever want to see it again. Just a damned bust-wing bird. . . ."

Still mumbling, tossed on swells of drunken pain, Justin blacked out again. Dan'l nodded at Web, who had been heating the finely honed edge of a big bone-handle knife with a heavy steel blade. The first part of the cut was fast and almost graceful. But Dan'l was forced to look away when Web's blade got caught up in bone and muscle. Justin was jolted awake by the pain, and Dan'l quickly slipped a strip of leather between his teeth. Without hesitation, he slugged his friend on the jaw, knocking him out.

"Thankee, Dan'l," Web said. He finished, and while Dan'l quickly cauterized the veins and arteries of the bleeding arm with a red-hot blade, Web flung the bloody and broken limb into the river.

Dan'l elevated the stump and wrapped it tight with linen strips. He knew that Justin was far from out of the woods. And the dark looks that Barry Woodyard and his minions cast at Dan'l meant there might be even more casualties before they reached Indian country.

Chapter Ten

For three more seemingly endless days, Sheltowee's Rangers pushed west-by-southwest along the briskly moving Ohio, making good time but driving farther into territory known only to Dan'l Boone and Web Finley. And even those two had never pushed deep into the Flat River Country of New Spain, where the first cache was located.

Sawyers presented no more major problems. But often the wind went against them, and most of the men spent long hours on the poles. Dan'l's square, weathered face was turned usually to either bank—and often, toward the far western horizon. There were treks out that way, Dan'l's glance seemed to say, that you won't read about in books. History a man can see with his inside eye. History that dies with him, unrecorded but real nonetheless.

Finally, they reached the juncture of the Ohio and the Mississippi. Using logs to roll their flatboat onto shore, the industrious Rangers stowed it in dense woods near the juncture. As for their horses, Dan'l had that part worked out already. Justin McQuady had made remarkable progress since his amputation, the wound already knitting soundly. One more night of rest, and Dan'l figured Justin would feel sassy enough to serve as hostler.

From his previous scouts, Dan'l knew of an excellent piece of graze about a mile east of the Mississippi. The steep back of a bluff, plus two dense thickets north and south, formed three natural walls of a huge pasture. While Justin spent one more day recuperating, the men hastily erected a line of poles to form the fourth side. The piece of available grass was generous and crossed by a little backwater creek. Dan'l figured about all Justin would really have to do is build night fires to scare off any wildcats and such that might attack the stock.

Dan'l called all the men together the night before they forded the Mississippi on crude rafts they had built earlier that day.

"Here's the way of it," he informed them. "Where we need to be ain't but a holler and a half from here. Trouble is, it's a rough piece of work to get there. It's low bottoms filled with dense thickets of cane. Them're separated by steep, rocky ridges. Only way through them canebrakes is to chop it down. It's tough and wiry, and grows so thick it'll dull your ax quicker 'n scat."

"The hell we do when we bust through it?" somebody hollered out. "Our hosses'll be back here."

"First off," Dan'l said, "let's see can we get through that cane in four days. Four nights, I mean, on account we'll be working nights, holing up days. Indians don't scout at night. I'm sending Webster a little south of here tomorrow after sunup. He's taking some riders, and they're going to make a false trail, make it look like we took off looking for the Warrior's Trace. We don't want no red sons knowing 'zacly where we're at.

"As for the horses . . . of those who ride south with Web, three men're staying back. On the third day, they take off down the trail we'll be hacking out, with our horses on lead lines. We stick to my plan, they'll be arriving just about the time we clear them 'brakes."

"What happens when we clear the cane?" O'Brien asked. "We just put our thumbs up our sitters?"

"I got a plan," Dan'l said enigmatically, not bothering to elaborate yet. "I'll spell it out better later."

Web kept mum in front of the others, but the moment he got Dan'l alone, he demanded, "*What* damn plan, Boone? I swan, you're the boy for holding your cards close."

"It's mighty puny as a plan," Dan'l admitted. For a moment, he glanced at a little musette bag he'd been guarding close since this expedition began. "Sort of a diversion, you might call it. Webster, we can't be risking three bloody battles to take them caches out reg'lar-like, one after the next. It's got to be done bold, and in one stroke."

"Ahuh. And every Jack shall have his Jill, too. Boone, have you et Johnson grass? We got twenty men—half of 'em still sprouts—and them caches is all wide separated! The hell you talkin,' a 'diversion'? Them red Arabs is gunna 'divert' our souls right outta our bodies!"

"Well, then, by God, we'll go to heaven and play cards with the Lord!" Dan'l exclaimed, slapping his comrade on the shoulder to rally him. "You mean to live forever, old fool?"

Web grinned. "Ahhh—you ain't got me kilt yet, Boone, for all your tryin'!"

Dan'l winked. By now his wound was almost closed, and he had his fighting fettle back. "Then, let's see can I do it this time. Speaking in general, old hoss, most men live too long as it is. Tell you true, I'm as worried about the weather as I am Injuns. You feel the snap to the air tonight?"

Web frowned, nodding. "Aye! We get caught in one a them late ice storms, them chowderheads will rue the day they ever got to 'vote.' They all called it swamp fog when you said we should wait a fortnight. Every man a Magellan! Huh. Hawg stupid is what they are."

The next night, while the moon arced toward its zenith in a star-shot sky, the Kentucky Rangers labored like beasts in the traces.

As planned, Web and several men had set out earlier to the south, then doubled back under dense cover. After sunset, the entire party, minus Justin and three men waiting with the horses, forded the Mississippi on rafts. Once they were across, ten miles of backwater swamps and thick woods made the first stretch rough, but manageable. Then the trees thinned out, and soon the men were forced to hack out a hard-won path through canebrake country.

This was not the jointed, bamboolike cane Dan'l had encountered in the Spanish territory of the Southeast. It was actually a very tough, wiry grass that grew higher than a tall man's head. Too dense to press through, it had to be laboriously cut—cut low, and then jerked out by hand to make sure it didn't grow back in days. But because it was so woodlike in substance, it needed an ax blade, not a scythe.

Dan'l organized labor teams, constantly shifting tasks to vary monotony. Four men cut the initial swathe while four men followed them to jerk loose the woody stems and toss them aside. Meanwhile, the other half of the men rested behind them, trading places each hour. It was grueling backbreaking labor, and only constant rest periods could allow a man to keep it up all night.

By the first sunrise after they'd forded the Mississippi, the men were dead on their feet. Every man's hands were blistered and bleeding, their muscles raw and throbbing. The hunters had jerked some venison during the layover at the river, and after a hasty meal, the men rolled into their blankets and slept the sleep of the just until Web and Dan'l roused them toward sundown the next day.

"Colder 'n a witch's tit," Barry Woodyard snarled as the messes fortified themselves with hot tea and cold venison.

It had gotten noticeably colder during the day, Dan'l noticed. "Bad storm's makin' up," he told the others. "Might turn into an ice storm before the night is over. If it does, my advice is keep right on a-workin'. That'll keep you warmer than anything else."

"Ice storm?" Lonnie Papenhagen repeated. "It's April, Colonel Boone! This ain't Hudson's Bay country."

"April is a pretty name for a girl," Dan'l replied. "And like a girl, it's powerful fickle."

"Shoo! It's cold, all right," Orrin Mumford scoffed. "Ain't no ice storms comin', though."

"Hope you fellers're right," Dan'l said. "I shorely do."

But as the work progressed, and the darkness deepened under a cloud-baffled sky, the skeptics were converted. At first, before the icy rains started, it was only cold—bitter cold, with winds whipping so hard a man had to shout to make himself heard. But Dan'l was right on one point—work was the antidote to cold. For a change, men looked forward to being on the hourly work crews, not the rest teams. Until they discovered that the discarded cane made an easy, hot fire for warming themselves.

Thus it went—one team up front, chopping down and uprooting the 'brakes, while a team behind provided light with their warming fires. It was tolerable for the first part of the night, even cheery for moments if a man could ignore the constant protest of tired muscles.

Now and then the men got a short respite where high, rock-strewn ridges or occasional, scant-grown hills separated the cane bottoms. At such times Dan'l scanned the terrain carefully in the feeble light to plot their progress on his mental maps.

"Any sign of red sons?" Web asked him at one point. It was so cold Dan'l could see Web's breath forming puffs.

"Nary a one that I can see. You?"

Web shook his head. But somehow, this realization was little comfort. Both men had learned a valuable saying: *When you see Indians, be careful. When you don't see them, be even more careful.* The turmoil of the so-called French and Indian War was now officially behind them. But not the smaller grudges and battles it had spawned. Nor the memory of entire tribes wiped out by the white man's pox, as it had wiped out the Rees and Blackfeet in the Far West territory. There nothing was left but ghost villages.

"Damn, it's cold!" Web exclaimed, holding his hands over the fire. "Lookit there, Dan'l," he added, nodding toward the spot downridge where Barry Woodyard sat with his minions. "That jackass just won't put a cork in it. Know what I heard from Judge Henderson? He ain't no man to speak agin others lightly. Yet he told me Barry was a debt-skipper back in the Carolina hills."

Dan'l nodded. "The judge tells it straight. I know of the Woodyards from way back. Debt skippers, horse-stealers, and barn-burners."

Web scowled, shivering as the wind gusted to a shriek. "By grab! I'd as lief shoot that kind as look at 'em! If that Barry was a cow, he'd be what they call a bunch-quitter. He's in it to win it—all for his ownself, the next feller be damned."

"Time is pushing," Dan'l said, wearily rising to his feet and grabbing his ax. "Let's do the same."

Before too long, just as Dan'l had feared, the rain started. And soon the slanting, freezing sheets turned to ice and sleet.

Dan'l's beard and shaggy hair were soon frozen solid, icicles dripping off them. Even with the constant swinging of his ax, the falling ice tore at his skin like rock salt fired from a blunderbuss.

Now warming fires were impossible, and therefore so was resting. The work crews doubled up, men cursing for a while until they were too miserable even for that. Soon all of them realized that fighting Indians would be the welcome part of this journey into Hell—assuming they survived long enough to ever hug with the enemy.

At one point, Barry Woodyard loosed a virulent string of curses and hurled his ax off into the cane.

"Count me out!" he roared above the steady

rattle of ice hitting the 'brakes. "We got a clear trail behind us, and I'm takin' it back! Who's with me?"

Light was dim, but Dan'l could see Woodyard staring in Evan's direction. And Dan'l could feel Evan wavering. He could feel *all* the men wavering. For a moment Dan'l's weariness, and the weight of command, caught up with him. Anger at Woodyard gripped him so tight it left his jaw aching.

The rain halted temporarily as a scud of clouds blew away from the moon. Everyone could see him when Dan'l hoisted his ax.

"I know this is a hell-buster, boys," Dan'l said, his voice clear but dangerously devoid of emotion. "Don't matter how you slice it, it's rough. But I'll make it even goddamn rougher for any white-livered, milk-kneed, disloyal bastard who tries to leave. Back to home, I picked only men as'd get 'er done. So *get* 'er done! Or kill me now, if you think you're man enough."

For a long minute, menace marked the very air. Dan'l and Woodyard squared off, facing each other, axes raised.

Suddenly, Web's old voice called out cheerfully, "Boys, God strike me down now if a mug of cold small beer wouldn't be just the fellow right about now. This is *fine* weather for a picnic, ain't it, though?"

And now, inspired by his father, Corey yelled out to Lonnie, "*Ain't* this the life, chappie?"

"Why, it's a broken drum," Lonnie replied. "Can't be beat!"

And Corey, having heard his old man tease

Dan'l for years, added, "Why, if Dan'l Boone can't get a man killed, then by God, he'll work him to death! What man could ask for more?"

Dan'l grinned, several men laughed, and others started working again despite their misery and suffering. Woodyard cursed, but went to retrieve his ax. Soon he was hacking away with the rest, his big, bluff face set tight with rage.

Chapter Eleven

War Hawk struck fire from a piece of flint with the ten-inch blade of his knife, igniting a little pile of crumbled-bark kindling. Soon a small council fire burned.

"Have ears for my words," the Shawnee battle leader told his companions. Anger was clear behind the level flatness of his voice, though he showed nothing in his face. "This is Boone's excellent treachery! How many times have I watched him do it? He lays low like a sated bear. He keeps to the woods and sleeps, rests, eats, and grows strong. Meanwhile, men's fears begin to work on them like ghost voices in the wind. *Where is Boone?* the voices whisper. Soon, like you two, they are jumping at shadows."

While War Hawk raged, Scalp Cane continued peeling a twig with his teeth, saying nothing. Iron Eyes, however, spoke out boldly.

"And you? The big warrior who fears no hair-face legend? You are not troubled by this seeming disappearance of Boone and his soldiers? Perhaps a wise man *would* be. Even Goes Ahead has lost them. You went too far when you left Boone's medal at that stone lodge to taunt him."

"This Boone shamed you," Scalp Cane added. "He made you wear the shawl up in Detroit. Now will we ruin the entire Red Nation so War Hawk can gorge on revenge for past slights? This Daniel Boone—some of the Headmen say he has sent word recently that he wishes to buy a private treaty. Perhaps the peace road is best with Sheltowee."

War Hawk was not one to brook such defiance from many men. But he feared that his Fox ally spoke straight words about the medal. It had seemed a stroke of genius at the time. But by leaving it with the dead, War Hawk had involved Boone directly in the massacre at Blackford's Mill. Sheltowee would not set foot in Kentucky again until that massacre was avenged. Therefore, War Hawk must not anger his battle cousins. He would need them.

"Of course I, too, am troubled," he confessed. "Only a fool takes Boone lightly. I do not call either of you cowards. Who among us has ever hidden in his lodge while his brothers struck the warpath?"

A bobcat's shrill kill-cry sounded from the surrounding hills, as if to emphasize the truth behind this boast. War Hawk began working a whetstone in smooth swipes along the blade of his knife.

"But turn this thing over and examine all of its facets," he continued. "Even now, with your foolish talk of the peace road with white men—that is Boone working on you! True, Boone cannot stop every fool from believing and repeating the legend of Sheltowee. But see how it is? Now that the legend is created, he slyly uses it to his advantage. That is why he has dropped out of sight. And now even our shamans are scaring the manhood from us!"

War Hawk, knowing how deeply most Indians respected magic, stopped short of actually ridiculing the ceremony conducted by Manitou earlier. With the braves' nerves unstrung by Boone's taunting silence, Manitou had blessed a basket filled with acorns. Now each brave, War Hawk included, carried a "magic acorn" in his private medicine bundle as a protection against Sheltowee. But War Hawk had spent several winters living at French and British outposts. He had lost much of his respect for the claims of magic. And he knew how whites could use it to control Indians.

"Never mind this clash of bulls among us!" War Hawk abruptly called out. He turned his knife to study the blade from another angle. "The Headmen have settled on a plan, and it is good enough for me."

"I like it, too," Iron Eyes agreed. "Especially the wisdom of keeping small groups near each cache while others patrol. This is wise when our quarry is out of sight."

The main cache, in the bluffs overlooking Flat River, was especially well guarded. Quick and elusive battle groups of eight and ten warriors were also patrolling this vast, often hostile and harsh land. The latest reports from runners and mirror flashes had been confusing and inconsistent—the truth was, no one knew with certainty where Boone was, or where, or when, he would appear.

"Remind your men," War Hawk said, "that I will give my fine new dappled gray *and* my English saddle to the man who takes Boone alive."

Scalp Cane spat out his twig. "Then why did you send permission for Goes Ahead to kill him on the river?"

"Because I knew he would fail! Boone is no immortal, bucks, but he will be harder to kill than that. Yet I also knew the attempt would unstring the nerves of some of Boone's warriors. It has also whetted the need of our men to see if Boone *is* the mighty legend."

Both of his companions understood this last point. There was more here than just War Hawk's great need to avenge his humiliation up in Detroit. For many tribes, torture was group entertainment. But for the Shawnees, it took on a religious and moral significance—it tested an enemy, measured his worth, proved whether or not the claims about his courage had substance behind them or only wind.

But War Hawk had something besides torture in mind. He glanced at his lethally honed blade, and thought again about Boone's own reputation as a blade fighter. He was the only man War Hawk knew of who preferred a curved skinning blade in a fight. Some claimed he was even better than the Cherokees' best knife fighter, Dragging Canoe. Truly, the brave who carved Boone's heart out would rule red men from here to the Land Beyond the Sun.

"I say it again," War Hawk declared with firm determination. "It is the same with *all* these whiteskin 'legends.' They are portrayed as violent men of action. Yet most often, they are mainly crafty. They know how to find and chip away at their enemy's weakness. Thus, the man with *no* weakness in him will gut Boone!"

"Well, I'm a Dutchman!" Dan'l exclaimed. "I *told* you we'd only need four nights. Lads, here's the Flat River!"

The men, worn down to the hubs, were too exhausted to raise a cheer. The last few miles of constant hacking and slashing had been especially rough. For hours, gnats had formed a maddening swirl in their faces, plugging their nostrils, irritating their eyes and bleeding sores.

But now the men crowded around Dan'l on a shale-littered ridge. Below, awash in ghostly silver-white moonlight, the Flat River reflected like black ice. The men from Kentucky had indeed finally cleared a trail through the arduous canebrakes and reached the tableland over the river.

"Why, hell's bells! That must be Henri Lasalle's old tradin' post!" Web said. He pointed toward some crumbling remains near the river, a crude structure of cottonwood logs and mud.

"Might's well pitch camp right here," Dan'l decided. "Make it a cold camp, though. And stay to the back side of the ridge. Come sunrise, there'll be red sons aplenty down below."

Men stamped their feet against the frigid air. Their mounts stood below them, prancing against the bitter cold. Justin and the three-man team from the Mississippi had arrived with them on the fourth day, as Dan'l had ordered. The ice storms were over, but not this lingering late-season cold wave.

"That was a easy trip with the cane cut down for us," Justin remarked. "Even seeing's how I only had one hand for the reins. But them hosses ain't grazed or watered since we left 'cept some of that cane you boys left 'side the trail. That's puny eatin'."

"We'll sneak 'em down to the river in relays during the night," Dan'l said. "But while we're up here, best keep their forelegs hobbled."

"What they really need," Web advised, "is some corn or oats. They've had good grass of late. But them hosses was grained all winter—they ain't used to nothin' but fodder."

"T'hell with mollycoddling the horses!" Woodyard complained. "What about *us*? No goddamn fires? It'll be a cold camp, all right."

"Set it to violin and mebbe I'll cry," Web shot back.

Dan'l and Web found a good spot in the lee of the wind and spread their ground sheets and blankets.

"Ain't just the horses is spoiled," Dan'l confessed. "I had me an easy winter. A man could get used to Becky's bacon and pan bread every morning."

"A man could get used to *every* thing about Becky," Web agreed. He watched Dan'l ground his breechloader next to that musette bag that Dan'l had been safeguarding since they left the settlements. Web eyed it again, squinting thoughtfully.

"Look here, Sheltowee. Where's this first cache?"

"A man could damn near see it from here in daylight," Dan'l assured him. "Up in the bluffs on the yonder side of the Flat. A big, dry, well-protected cave. Or that's how it's told, anyhow, by some that know."

"Ahuh. Or *say* they know." But Web knew Dan'l too well by now to have any serious doubts on this matter.

"The thing of it is," Dan'l went on in his easy drawl, "what's said to be inside all three them caches. Something what'll make burning 'em easier than rolling off a log. Quicker, too."

Web's creased-leather brow furrowed even deeper in a frown. "Them bastards usin' black powder now?"

"Something they've had even longer. Got it from the French while even *you* were still a tad, Methuselah. Matter fact, it's something that's been around since them ancient Greeks done battle with those Trojans. My pap used to call it Greek fire."

"Gun-cotton!" Web exclaimed.

Dan'l nodded. "I'm told they got kegs of nitre and sulphur and such from the French. Plus bolts of tow cloth to soak it up. One man with a good flint-and-steel could bring down the whole shivaree."

Web was busy removing pieces of shale from the dirt under his bed. "It's God's truth," he mused, "they're wild over gun-cotton. But damn it all, Boone! You yourself said them 'ere caches is well pertected. Them red Arabs, why, mayhap they've gone to breastworks! Now, the British butchers under King George would just put in wave after wave till it was done, never mind the widows and orphans it made. I reckon it won't take you long a'tall to kill us twenty."

Dan'l glanced again at the musette bag, hoping he wasn't erecting his hopes on a foundation of air. The next moment he sat up, for he saw Lord Dunmore's head come up and his ears prick forward. Probably just fidgety in new country, Dan'l figured.

"You just simmer down, old-timer," Dan'l told Web. "You already got us all planted in the bone orchard! It's a tricky piece of work, I'll grant you. It'll have to be done just right. First off, we got to let them red aboriginals know we're here."

Web goggled at him in the wan moonlight. "Let them—Air ye daft, lad? Deliberate-like? Let them know a-purpose?"

"Did I speak Chinee? A-purpose, yessir. But that force we let 'em see, led by you, will just be a decoy."

"Lord, I'm a-scairt to ask. A decoy for what?"

Dan'l sent Web a sign to wait a bit. Then he started down the ridge toward the horses. Lord Dunmore was still sniffing the wind.

"What's on the spit, old trooper?" Dan'l said to his favorite mount, giving him a good scratch along the withers. "You in a fret over them hobbles, uh?"

Dan'l glanced all around them in the cold darkness, trying to distinguish shadow from form. Lord Dunmore was ugly, Dan'l conceded, but with impressive muscle conformation and powerful haunches. Most white men spirit-broke their horses when they trained them to leather—choking, water-starving, using wire bits that cut their mouths when they rebelled.

But like a man, a horse *needed* spirit. None of Dan'l Boone's horses had ever known a breaking saddle. He broke them in the style of the great horse tribes in the short-grass country—he simply jumped on and rode until the horse was exhausted. If he was still on when the animal finally stopped, Dan'l was the master.

But sometimes, too much spirit made a horse extra skittish. Dan'l scratched Lord Dunmore behind the ears. Still, though he saw no sign of trouble, Dan'l decided to rescind the order on hobbling the horses. Ground-tethering would be good enough. He didn't realize, just then, how that decision would save their lives before the night was over.

The attack came suddenly, the way death often arrived on the frontier.

During the night the horses had been led down to the Flat River to graze and water. Finally, about two hours before dawn, the animals were returned to the camp on the ridge. The men settled in for a brief stint of well-earned sleep.

Dan'l wasn't sure exactly what woke him up first—the angry snarling or the frightened nickering of the horses. But he came up from the blankets with his short iron to hand and glanced down at the horses.

They were bucking, jackknifing, crowhopping wildly, trying to defend themselves from a snarling pack of gray wolves! At first, as he squeezed his trigger to scare the intruders off, Dan'l actually felt relief. Wolves were far better than Indians—they would not press the attack once men got into it.

But the moment his flintlock pistol exploded, the ravenous pack whirled, and Dan'l realized the rovers from Kentucky were all in a world of hurt. For the pack leaders were wild dogs. Wild dogs were more dangerous than wolves. The wolf still had its instinctive fear of man, but the wild dog had nearly lost his fear due to earlier domestication. So its fury was not tempered by the man smell.

Many of the men were not even awake yet when, fast as a finger snap, the predators were on them. There was little chance for any shooting. It was a savage fight with axes, knives, muskets turned into clubs—whatever a man could get to hand before one of the beasts was on him, searching for purchase on his throat.

But their arms were stiff with cold and exhaustion, and the wolves and dogs were tenacious in their attack. Dan'l cracked one on the skull with the butt of his breechloader, then almost fell to the ground as a second animal leaped into his chest like a gray cannonball.

Dan'l had watched wolves at work in buffalo herds. By instinct, they went for a prey's tendons to disable it. Dan'l danced around and around, keeping a wolf's snapping teeth away from the backs of his knees. He also resisted the temptation to throw up his arms to protect his face—that exposed the tendons inside the elbows. Tendons didn't heal. Once they were severed, a man was ruined past helping.

Men cursed, injured wolves and dogs yelped, and now and then a man howled in pain as tooth or claw sank into flesh. But in an instant, as quickly as it began, the pack flew off over the ridge, leaving a few dead and stunned comrades behind.

At first it looked like the militiamen would come out of it with nothing more than a few bites and scratches. But then a muffled curse from Web brought the men to the spot where one-armed Justin McQuady's bed had become his grave.

Justin lay in a blood-soaked heap. His throat had been torn completely open, and an expression of horrified pain was frozen on his face. Disabled as he was, Dan'l realized, the poor fellow had never had a chance.

"All right," Dan'l said with quiet determination. "The Injuns around here have heard my shot. They won't ride out till sunrise, but that ain't long from now. Evan, Web! Pick two men each from your squad and dig a grave for Justin.

Make sure you burn gunpowder over it to keep the varmints from diggin' him up. The rest, stoke your bellies and get set to ride."

Dan'l turned away. But some of the men were still staring at Justin's terrified death rictus, as if fascinated.

"I ain't talking to hear my own voice!" Dan'l snapped. "I give an order, and I expect it to be carried out. The dyin' ain't over yet, so no need to be staring now like you never saw a corpse. You'll see more dead men before I'm done with you."

Chapter Twelve

As soon as Justin was in the ground, the men prayed over him and prepared to move out. A sentry remained atop the ridge during all this. Soon Dan'l noticed that glow in the east like foxfire, the light some called false dawn. It meant the real thing was nigh.

"Prepare to mount!" he called out. "But listen up first. This sport coming up is why we tested you. From here on out, it's your shooting and riding skills that matter. On account of the numbers we're up against, there'll be *no* defensive positions. You can't kill an Indian until you fight like an Indian. So we stay in motion, hit and run. This ain't no 'standing army,' it's rangers. We'll be fightin' hard and ridin' hard, and it'll be a bloody piece of work before it's behind us."

Dan'l gave it to them with the bark still on it, rough and raw and untouched. Evan Blackford, Lonnie Papenhagen, and a few others seemed to welcome Dan'l's grim frankness. The massacre of the Blackford and Hopewell families had determined their course—only death would stop them now. Others, like Barry Woodyard and his toady, Stone Ludlow, had the uneasy look of men who had bought a lame horse while drunk, and now wanted their money back.

"We strike first," Dan'l went on. "And we strike hard. Indians read sign like breathin', so we don't dare make no camps for more than a few hours, and then only with picket outposts."

"Strike first?" Ludlow objected. "Agin a force that big?"

"It's big if you put it all together in your head. But I'll wager it's broke up into scouting parties right now, watching for us."

"You're mighty quick to wager," Woodyard said, "with our lives."

Corey whirled on the older man and demanded, "How many arrows you had shot in *you* so far?"

"You little squirt, I—"

"Ease off, both of you," Dan'l snapped. "You can kill each other later. Right now time's pushing. Let me speak my piece so we can ride out. My plan is just sorter scratched in the dirt, see. It's got two parts. The first part calls for us to get them red sons bunched here around the bluffs. As many as we can draw to the area. And we need to *keep* 'em here. But an empty hand is no lure for a hawk. So we attack one or two patrols. Shoot 'em to rag tatters!"

"And then the rest'll be all over us like ugly on a buzzard," Woodyard carped. "How you plan to get at them caches you been harpin' on, when we got half the consarn red nation on our hinders?"

"That's the second part of my plan," Dan'l replied. "And we ain't got there yet, y'unnerstan'?"

Again Woodyard and Ludlow started to object. But it was Web, hiding a sly smile behind his hand, who answered. For the old trapper had taken a peek inside Dan'l's closely guarded musette bag.

"Daniel Boone's chief, principal, and primary skill," Web growled, "is in helpin' a man get his half-penny life over quick. So it's best to glimpse his plans in little peeks, Mr. Woodyard, same way you might look into the sun. That way, you won't see 'zacly when you're bound to die!"

Despite the tension, there was an explosion of laughter at this. Leaving Woodyard to scowl and mutter, Dan'l went through the final preparations for battle. He checked his saddle and pad for burrs; he carefully examined the cinches, latigos, stirrups; finally he checked the halter and reins. He cut a few fringes from his buckskin shirt and used them to mend a weak spot in one of the cinches. Then he saddled Lord Dunmore.

All around Dan'l, similar preparations went forward with a somber practicality. Men filled their shot pouches and powder flasks and horns. Dan'l watched Orrin Mumford attach the long, thin bayonet to his British Ferguson gun. Evan Blackford tucked a hatchet into his sash, his young face set hard with purpose.

In the quiet, chilly, predawn mist, it was hard for Dan'l to accept that men were about to die. Men he knew and soldiered with, maybe himself. And there was a good chance the death would not be sudden and merciful, but slow and grueling over a fire that cooked a man alive for hours. Dan'l had found remains of Indian torture fires, the brains still bubbling in the hot skulls of their victims.

Dan'l thought these things while he listened to the scolding of jays, the snorting of horses, the chink of bit rings and creak of leather as men rigged their mounts. Then, even as the first glorious, roseate blush of dawn appeared in the east, came the warning Dan'l had been expecting.

"Innuns!" the sentry on the ridge called down. "Ten, twelve of 'em, down by the river!"

"Grab leather, Rangers!" Dan'l ordered. "Stay in motion so's you don't make an easy bead. If your horse is hit, get your legs up quick so's you ain't pinned when it drops. And remember, one bullet, one Indian!"

The men from Kentucky rode boldly over the crest of the ridge in two columns at close intervals. Dan'l spotted the Indians immediately, riding single file on the west bank of the Flat, just below the rocky bluffs. Dan'l recognized the tricolored plumes of Shawnees.

"War Hawk among 'em?" Web asked, for he had never seen the renegade battle chief.

"Not this bunch," Dan'l replied. "See there, where the river oxbows?" Dan'l pointed north, so all his men could see where he meant. A magnificent cataract tumbled down from atop a limestone cliff in an explosion of white foam. "Word has it the main cache is right above that waterfall. I'll wager them red sons below us was camped near there all night.

"Evan!" Dan'l shouted. "Take your squad wide on the right flank, and give me a little lead before you ride full-bore. Web, you swing your boys wide left and do the same. Both of you, wait till most a them redskins're watching me. Then close together in a pincers. *Gee* up, Lord Dunmore!"

Dan'l heeled the big, ugly roan, and they leaped forward, "splitting the flanks," as Dan'l called it when he drew first fire as a distraction between two points of a pincers—one of his favorite fighting strategies against Indians.

The Flat River was narrow and shallow there, with gravel bars that provided excellent fording. Dan'l, with less distance to cover, was first to draw within range of the enemy; he had nearly gained the river before the Indians, intent on studying their side of the water, noticed him. Though surprised at suddenly being on the defensive, they decided to fight rather than flee.

Dan'l already knew they would never dismount and take up positions, white-man style, among the rocks and bushes. Indians seldom forted up, and they followed little group discipline in a battle, relying on individual courage and initiative to inspire others at key moments. Even as Lord Dunmore hurtled into the river, Dan'l brought his breechloader to the ready. The primer popped, the main charge exploded, and Dan'l felt the big gun buck hard in his hands. A Shawnee raised his surprised face toward heaven when the ball knocked a hole in his chest, spinning him sideways off his pony.

Dan'l and Lord Dunmore had a full head of steam behind them. They hurtled right through the Shawnees, the roan easily clearing the fallen Indian in a leap.

In his right eye, Dan'l saw a brave hurl something at him. Dan'l flattened himself over his horse's neck just as the war lance shot over him, its stone tip missing by inches.

Even as Lord Dunmore pounded up the sloping west bank, Dan'l balanced his long gun across his lap. He clawed his flintlock pistol from the holster, slewed around awkwardly in the saddle, and shot the nearest brave low in his guts.

By now the Kentucky riders were pounding close from both flanks, and not a moment too soon by Dan'l's reckoning. Their deep curses and war cries contrasted starkly with the yipping clamor of the Indians. But Dan'l knew the element of surprise was now played out. Despite being outnumbered, the Indians had one distinct advantage: They could launch as many as a dozen arrows while their whiteskin enemies charged their "barking irons."

Dan'l took up a Plains Indian battle position,

swinging to one side and clutching the horse's neck, shielding his body with the animal's. A flurry of deadly, fire-hardened arrows turned the air lively all around Dan'l. He felt Lord Dunmore shudder as an arrow nicked him in the side, sending up a puff of dust. The blow was not fatal, but it broke the animal's rapid stride.

Two braves, finally recognizing the mighty Sheltowee, surged forward to seize him before his horse could regain momentum. Dan'l, with no time to reload either of his guns, seized the knife from his right moccasin and whirled to meet the attack.

But he was just in time to watch the men from Kentucky do him proud. Young Corey Finley raised his fowling piece, fired an offhand shot, and one Shawnee's face disappeared in a red smear. Lonnie Papenhagen, farther back, opted to drop the second Indian's pony. But Evan Blackford finished the job, riding in close to open the warrior's breastbone with his hatchet.

"Stay in motion!" Dan'l screamed. "Keep movin'! It ain't no turkey shoot, don't give 'em a bead on you!"

But Orrin Mumford, dizzy with the elation that accompanies early luck in a battle, grew too confident that this was a rout. Dan'l watched him rein in his big seventeen-hand gray to lay a bead on a Shawnee.

"Orrin!" Dan'l hollered, so loud the word seemed to claw his throat. "Orrin, don't—"

The warning snagged in Daniel's throat as he watched a swarm of arrows suddenly seem to sprout from Orrin's big body. Roaring in death agony, blood spewing from several fatal hits, Orrin crashed to the ground like a sack of meal.

But the Shawnees were unable to turn the battle against this disciplined and determined force. Nor could they easily flee—high banks led to a steep ridge on the east, to the rocky bluffs on the west. The remainder tried to escape north, following the river, but were quickly run down and slaughtered by the Kentucky riders.

"Why, it's money for old rope!" Web gloated as he caught up to Dan'l. "I seen how Corey and Lonnie pulled your bacon outta the fire, Boone! Them tads was *some,* Dan'l! Evan, too."

"They fought like she-bears. But this ain't no damn time to recite our coups, old son. Look yonder!"

Web followed Dan'l's pointing finger, up to the bluffs overhead. A line of at least fifty painted braves was streaming down from the rocks.

"Well, damn your bones, Sheltowee!" Web exclaimed. "You wanted redskins on our tail, di'n you? Here they come! You happy now, you soft-brained son of trouble?"

Dan'l roared out to the men ahead of them, calling them back. He considered gathering up Orrin's body, but his horse had scattered. Dan'l couldn't strap any man with extra weight, not considering the hard fleeing they had ahead of them. Orrin's body would be terribly mutilated by the outraged Indians pouring down at them, but Dan'l knew there was no help for it.

"Hell, yes, I'm happy!" he shouted to Web, matching bluff for bluff. "No Boone wants to die of old age. Now stick a stopper on your gob and make tracks, Webster!"

Chapter Thirteen

These tribes were new to the western lands and the new hunting ranges farther northwest from the Flat River. Dan'l was counting on that as he ordered the direction for what he termed a "fighting retreat."

To the east, past the river and the razorback ridge where they'd buried Justin, lay the cane-brake country. Fleeing that way meant revealing their escape trail. True, Indians would not long pursue them on a strange trace, especially one so hemmed in on all sides—no red man could abide confinement. But they would guard that trail opening at their end with their lives, and Sheltowee's Rangers would have no choice but to return east, their mission a failure, the settlements unprotected.

The country due north, Dan'l knew from

studying trappers' maps, was hilly and wooded. But to the south, it was mostly open grassland with scattered pine trees and low, sandy hills.

So Dan'l led his force south, keeping them in staggered columns to minimize chance hits during enfiladed fire from behind. The force from Kentucky was still well in sight by the time the first Indian riders cleared the bluffs and gave chase.

Dan'l and Web had both fought Indians enough to know how they despised any enemy, red or white, who ran. But an enemy who fought well while running deserved respect—that was why Dan'l had chosen this open country. If it made the quarry an easier target, that meant the hunters, too, were more vulnerable.

The Indian ponies, though good mustang stock, had passed a hard winter in Spanish Missouri. They'd survived by grazing on cottonwood bark and by breaking through the snow crust to eat the brown, stunted grass beneath. The new grass had not been up long enough to put meat back on their flanks or the vital, quickening light in their eyes when they galloped.

The Kentucky horses, however, had been lightly used so far. Winter graining had left these "American horses," as the French and some tribes called them, sleek and well nourished. Too, they averaged sixteen hands as against fourteen for Indian mounts. The sure-footed ponies, at a definite advantage in mountain terrain, were nonetheless a bit slower in open country.

That did not prevent their Indian pursuers,

however, from keeping up a deadly harassment fire with their strongest bows. Some of these were made from the wood of the osage tree, brought out of the southwest by Kiowa Apache traders. When strung with the best buffalo sinew, these could hurl arrows an incredible 1200 yards.

Two men were wounded, neither seriously, by the time the Rangers finally opened up a safe lead on their enemy. But Dan'l had recognized War Hawk leading them—there was no missing that ugly damn scar of his. That meant this present lead would not last long unless Dan'l slowed those savages down by taking some spirit out of them.

"Take the lead," Dan'l told Web when the force stopped briefly to water at a small pond fed by a rill. "I'll be dropping back for a spell."

Web saw that their horses were all blowing foam from the hard run. He nodded, knowing what his friend had in mind.

"Godspeed, Sheltowee," Web told him. "Watch 'em arrahs. And gitcher wind right, boy."

It was a risky, but often effective, technique Dan'l had perfected in the open country south of Santa Fe. He watched the other men ride out. Then he took up the drag. He held Lord Dunmore back from a full gallop, making it appear to those behind him that his horse was finally winded.

Dan'l knew that, by now, War Hawk knew damn well which rider was Sheltowee. That meant that by strict order no one would be firing at him—not so long as it appeared there was a chance to take him alive.

Dan'l continued to fall back. His breechloader was primed and ready. It was sighted for game at about two hundred yards. Dan'l waited until he could hear the Indian ponies snorting behind him. Then he went into fast action.

With a hard tug on the left rein, he wheeled his big roan around 180 degrees and halted him by tossing the reins out over his ears. Dan'l instantly drew his back lower against the cantle while he hooked his left knee around the saddlehorn. That gave him a fairly secure rest for the muzzle of his long gun.

"Steady, Lord Dunmore," he muttered. "This'll singe your ears a mite, is all."

All this had taken only seconds. War Hawk was only now reacting to the danger. Dan'l drew a quick bead on War Hawk, fired, but missed. The explorer cursed, realizing wind drift had caught him despite Web's warning to compensate.

But he kept a steady hand and resolute heart. He had watched men get rattled under pressure, start repeating useless actions over and over, their competence turned to useless panic. Most of them were dead now.

"Steady as bedrock, boy," he soothed his horse, who had sidestepped at the shot.

Dan'l shook powder into the pan of his breechloading musket. Seeing him just start to reload, War Hawk calculated the time needed and charged even faster. But Dan'l had paid a gunsmith in New Orleans to modify the flintlock. In its original version, very little speed was gained over muzzle-loaders, since the breech-plug required a wrench. Dan'l had it tooled so he could remove it with a thumb and forefinger.

Now he could get up to four shots a minute, whereas a good shot with a muzzle-loader might get two. War Hawk thudded closer, a murderous horde behind him, as Dan'l thumbed a ball past the loading gate.

Dan'l deliberately lowered this shot, tagging War Hawk's pony with a wound to the right foreleg. With impressive agility, the warrior lifted both legs, pivoted on his buffalo-hide saddle, and leaped onto the back of the nearest brave's pony, all before his own horse had stumbled hard to the ground.

Not exactly magic guiding his bullets, Dan'l realized as he whirled Lord Dunmore and raced to join his comrades. But some of the Indians had looked surprised—few white men with fire sticks could score hits at such a distance. But War Hawk had not looked surprised—only determined.

Soon, Dan'l realized, would come part two of his scratched-in-the-dirt plan. The hard part.

"Every man-jack one of you did his job," Dan'l announced to the others. " 'Cept for you, Ludlow."

Toward the middle of the long afternoon, Dan'l had sent out two picket guards and ordered a halt to spell the exhausted horses. War Hawk and his group had turned back, no doubt to meet in hasty council and decide their next move.

Now, Stone Ludlow, busy scraping weevils off a square of saleratus bread, looked up startled. A westward bend in the Flat had placed the men close to the river once again. The force had tethered their mounts in a patch of good graze surrounded by coarse-barked cottonwoods.

"Me?" Ludlow demanded in his whiny hillman's twang. "The hell'd I do?"

"Not a damn thing," Dan'l replied. "In the attack back at the bluffs, you held back and fired your weapon into the air. And you ain't pitched in yet for the running battles."

"Well, back to the bluffs? My piece just went off accidental-like when my horse—"

"You're a liar," Boone said calmly. "A goddamn shirking, cowardly liar. You volunteered to be with this mission, nobody impressed you into service. I won't abide a malingering coward, y'unnerstan'? Our lives depend one upon the other. From here on out, either you pull your freight, or I'll put you under as an example to the rest."

Ludlow swallowed so hard his Adam's apple leaped. Boone looked mighty big right then, looming over him as he was. Mighty big, and mighty damned determined.

"Yessir," Ludlow muttered.

Barry Woodyard was one of Ludlow's mess partners. Dan'l turned to meet his unblinking, gunmetal eyes.

"Ain't no love betwixt us, Barry," Dan'l said quietly. "Matter fact, we may scrap again. But you're a stout lad when the war whoop sounds. I've watched ye. It does beat all that a man with the leather in him to fight like you can would abide a nancy like Stone here."

Ludlow's face twisted with hate, while Woodyard's jaw dropped open in pure astonishment. Dan'l, nodding thoughtfully, turned and walked away. Web pretended to choke on his jerked venison to disguise an admiring laugh at Dan'l's savvy. Dan'l, thinking only of the mission, recognized that Woodyard was a top-notch fighter. And driving a wedge between him and Ludlow was the best way to ensure Woodyard's cooperation for the bad trouble ahead.

Web just hoped to Jesus that Dan'l knew what he was doing. Ludlow might be a shirker, all right. But Woodyard was definitely dangerous, and the grudge light was in his eye.

Dan'l addressed all the men again. "The first part of the plan came off without a hitch, though we lost a good man to his own foolishness. The main mile is, I made sure to show myself. You seen all the smoke sign that went up earlier from the bluffs? *This* coon'll wager that's callin' the rest of the Injuns back to this area. War Hawk figures by now that we mean to either brace their main camp or hit that biggest cache. He can't even know for sure what we're up to."

"What *are* we up to, Colonel Boone?" young Steve Kitchens asked. "We can't touch that main cache. And the other two is a long ride from here."

"Evan Blackford is one of our best riders," Dan'l replied. "After dark, him and me ride hard. We kill any sentries left at those other caches. Then we burn them out. Meantime, you boys back here. . . ."

Still speaking, Dan'l began to unbuckle his heavy gunbelt. "You boys back here got clear title to Hell. Cuz you got the job of keeping up what we started today. You got to keep War Hawk thinking that Sheltowee and his bunch of hair-face fools are right here."

"How we do that?" Corey said doubtfully. "You won't be here."

Dan'l stopped in front of Barry Woodyard again and handed the surprised man his gunbelt.

"Boone'll be here," Dan'l said, "in body, if not in spirit. On account Barry's gonna be me. He'll ride my horse, he'll wear my gunbelt, he'll wear my flap hat. Barry's my size, got the same color beard."

"H'ar now!" Woodyard objected. "Boone, this ain't no time for none of your damned parlor tricks! We're up to our armpits in Injins. We need—"

"Barry," Dan'l said in his easy way. "No one asked you to put your oar in my boat. I give the orders, and you'll take 'em."

"But Colonel Boone," Lonnie said. "Even if you 'n' Evan can wipe out them other caches, how we spoze to get at thissen richeer by the river? Redskins're thicker 'n' ticks on a buff."

Web caught Dan'l's eye and grinned. Dan'l glanced at the musette bag tied to his rigging.

"Colt, there's thing even ticks won't abide," Dan'l replied, hoping he was right. "Webster! I'm volunteerin' your claybank for this ride.

Barry's hoss is good flesh, but I don't—"

"—trust a pretty horse," Web finished for him. "Might's well leave that damn Mexer saddle behind, too, Dan'l. That fancy silver trim'll catch sunlight and get you scalped."

Woodyard quit scowling and buckled on Dan'l's belt. Evan, looking glad to have this dangerous assignment, began checking his weapons.

"Now, take a care, Dan'l," Web warned when his claybank sidestepped away as Dan'l reached for the bridle. "He's still some deal wild. Some hosses'll fight the saddle, others save it for the rider. He'll try to buck any new rider. But he's a pattern bucker."

Dan'l nodded, understanding. A pattern bucker could be guessed and its leaps anticipated. Horses like Lord Dunmore, in contrast, were notional buckers that couldn't be predicted.

"He'll get another hour's rest and graze," Dan'l said, judging the slant of the shadows. "And then another hard ride."

"I reckon it's got to be did," Web mused. He pointed toward Woodyard, who had donned Dan'l's black wool hat. "By the Lord Harry! Look at him primp! That sour-faced groat *does* look like Sheltowee, from afar off. He's already grinnin', lookit there! Bein' the ramrod has gone to his head."

Dan'l nodded. His strong white teeth flashed through his beard when he smiled. "One thing *ain't* got to his head yet. He'll turn puny-green when it does, uh?"

Web laughed, for he too had just realized this. "Ahuh! Ol' Barry's forgettin' something. He ain't just playin' the head hound. He's turned hisself into the most wanted white man in the entire Red Nation."

Chapter Fourteen

Word came from a picket sentry that Indians, faces greased for battle, were approaching. Sheltowee's Rangers pushed on to a new site atop a low ridge that offered good visibility in all directions. But Dan'l meant it when he said there would be no sieges or "last stand" battles. Other than grouping their horses on the far side of the ridge, no defenses were erected.

"We spell the horses and see how they mean to play it," Dan'l explained. "Stoke your bellies while you can."

Two Indian ponies were shot, the second one a kill, before the war party halted, content for now to observe from a distance. When the sun was a round, dull orange ball low in the western sky, the Indians simply faded back toward their camp near the Flat River bluffs.

An hour after that, the dull orange ball exploded in a final salute of brilliant glory, then disappeared in darkness. The main group of Boonesborough Rangers pushed on to the southwest. They intended to move in constant circles, first in one direction, then the other, keeping that main cache as a sort of hub.

By now Dan'l and Web had worked out the kind of plan that Dan'l Boone always seemed to have trouble avoiding—one bold and chockablock with risks, a plan that went straight to the heart of a problem and did nothing by halves. A plan, in short, that might leave widows and orphans aplenty back in the settlements. But a man who didn't risk big, Dan'l firmly believed, couldn't win big either.

Dan'l and Evan rode out bearing northwest. Dan'l hoped his mental map was accurate and they were following near the Warrior's Trace. By his reckoning, it lay beyond a distant fall line to his left, a spot where natural drainage caused a huge trough to form. Old French and Russian trappers called that the Missouri Sink. Dan'l had used it, with the stars and a few other prominent land features, as his reference points throughout this expedition.

Boone estimated forty miles riding before they reached that next cache on the old French Lick branch of the Missouri. As for any Indians they might encounter in this unfamiliar country—the warriors would not, Dan'l reasoned, eagerly leave their camp circles after dark, believing their good magic lost its power without the life-giving sun. Nonetheless, they would eagerly violate many taboos in order to snare Sheltowee, the arch enemy of the Shawnee—and no red saint to the Foxes or Sauks either, Dan'l mused.

"There's Indians scattered around where we'll be riding," Dan'l warned Evan. "And the devil's own work to avoid 'em. So keep a bean in the tube in case we need to burn powder quick. We got to move like antelope, boy. Won't be no time for getting the lay of the land first."

But despite Dan'l's desperation to make good time, Web's claybank and Evan's big blood bay had been pushed too hard lately on nothing but fodder. Reluctantly, Dan'l decided to spell them regularly—every hour, both riders dismounted and walked their horses for ten minutes or so.

Even so, generous moonlight and a silver peppering of bright stars made for plenty of good riding. Dan'l guided them by a distant headland between the Pole Star and the Dog Star. The night air eventually chilled them to shivers, and at daybreak the grass on the open stretches was frosted and crunched under their horses' hooves.

They kept riding in the gathering light, taking that risk, pushing through some pretty country: wide meadows of blue columbine, and little hollows sheltered by pines. They were cutting across a wooded ridge when a sudden downpour sent gray sheets of water hurling toward them out of the distance. The two men were forced to shelter briefly in an old bear den.

Other times, later on, water was scarce, and they sucked on pebbles. Once Dan'l spotted a place near a river where Indians had set up racks to smoke fish. Toward mid-morning, as they drew near the next cache site, the two ravenous men raided a few of their enemy's rabbit snares and cooked up their first hot meal in a spell, using green wood that barely smoked.

"I know your blood's up to hit that cache," Dan'l told Evan during their hasty meal. "But this old coon needs sleep first. Soon as we've et, we rest a spell. They ain't likely to just *hand* that cache over, lad. It's likely to be a fight, and I ain't up to fettle."

"Me neither," Evan confessed. "I'm bushed, Mr. Boone. And we still got another hard ride to that last cache."

"Not 'we,' sprout. You're standing guard over this one while I ride north alone."

Evan started to object, but Dan'l held up a scorched joint of rabbit meat and shook it to silence him. "Don't fret none—yours ain't no feather-bed job, you may well get your chance to die, Evan. This thing's got to be done right! After we kill the sentries, you'll have to stay with the cache. You'll watch close for smoke north of here—that'll be the third cache going up after I fire it. Only then can you torch thissen, y'unnerstan'? Both of 'em at the same time. Elsewise, red devils might come a-swarmin' before all three are ruint. I say all three, for if things've gone right with Web's bunch, that third cache'll be sending up smoke soon after yours does."

Evan nodded slowly, seeing the sense of this plan. "I'll hold on long's I can," he said with brave resolution. "I ain't scairt to die, not after what they done to my own! But one man with a musket won't amount to a hill of beans if a passel of redskins show up after you ride out. How in the devil do I stop 'em? And though Web's got the main gather, won't that Flat River cache be heavy-guarded?"

"If we all use our think-pieces and show some spunk," Dan'l replied, digging into his musette bag, "mayhap we won't have to stop 'em. Not by ourselves, anyhow. Here, look at this, tadpole."

He tossed something into the grass in front of the youth. Evan started to pick it up. Then he saw what it was, and his hand snapped back as if he'd burned it.

"Golly-Bill!"

Evan crab-scuttled away from the object, staring at it in fascinated disgust. "What *is* that, Mr. Boone? Or I mean, *who* was it? Sweet Mary, he was an ugly cuss!"

"It's a shrunk-up human head," Dan'l replied matter-of-factly. "Bought it from a sailor at Congo Square down in N'awlins. Can't tell you who the gent was, though. Now these here—"

Dan'l pulled some crude stick-and-hair dolls out of the bag. They were simple, yet somehow sinister, painted with bright, odd symbols and staring out of black-button eyes.

"These here is called Juju men. Little African devil fellers. Little cousins to Satan or some such, I reckon. It's all heap-big Creole magic downriver. They call it Obeah."

Evan looked pale around the mouth. He refused to look at that hideous, long-haired, wrinkled-up head. Damn thing was no bigger than his fist!

"You're a Christian, ain'tcha?" Evan said doubtfully. "You don't credit that jungle magic, do you, Dan'l?"

Dan'l grinned despite his exhaustion. "Not only a Christian, boy, but one who reads the Book. But you see, it don't matter what *this* child believes. These is pagans. Way down south? Some sell these as gimcracks and gew-gaws, others believe they're powerful medicine. Some believe both—they're a mite queer down thataway and like to toss all their religions into one hotchpot.

"But these redskin pagans we're up agin? Why, they all know about Obeah. And it frights 'em, frights 'em bad, gives 'em the fantods. See thissen?"

Dan'l showed Evan a little sisal pouch filled with painted snake teeth. "Why, Web'd call it pee doodles. Nothin' to it. But I flashed it at a Shawnee working a barge on the Colbert. That red son like to died of fright right there."

"Here's one time I can't hardly blame the Injuns," Evan admitted. "Gives me belly flies just lookin' at all this truck. Somethin' . . . evil about it."

By now the two men had found a little spruce copse. They ground-hitched their mounts, then slipped the bits and loosed their cinches. The two men pushed drooping spruce branches aside and bedded down on a deep mat of fragrant needles within.

"How close you figure that cache to be?" Evan

asked as he waited for exhaustion to claim him.

"Only a fox-step away," Dan'l assured him. "You been fixin' the route in your mind like I told you?"

But Evan didn't hear the question. "They killed my entire family," Evan said wonderingly, surprising Dan'l. "I ain't got nobody left in this world. Don't hardly matter if I am killed."

"It'll matter plenty to that gal you spark back at the settlement."

"Libbie Sanford?"

"Aye. She's peart."

Evan's voice took on a new tone. "She ain't too hard to look at, is she? Sweet 'un, too. You should meet her, Dan'l."

"I hope to, son. She's more than worth goin' back for, I'd say. A man's got to live for something besides settlin' of scores. The trouble with revenge thirst—once you slake it, you got nothin' left. Now go to sleep. We got some rough plowin' ahead."

After a minute, Evan said, "Dan'l? Becky is worth goin' back for, too."

"Trooper, Becky is the reason I *came* here. Her and the tads. Now don't be slopping over. Pipe down and get you some sleep."

Dan'l never slept with one eye open. He had learned that a man who survives has to sleep deep when it's time. But the same trail discipline woke him just when the sun was on the verge of beginning its late-day descent. He was fully awake in a blink, rising and parting branches aside, his eyes already tracking along the horizons for trouble. He shook Evan, then stretched his muscles to work at the kinks a bit. Dan'l had spent the winter sleeping on a feather tick, with Becky there to soften things even more. This unforgiving ground was poor shakes by comparison.

Dan'l caught up the claybank and threw on the pad and saddle. He cinched the girth tight under his belly. Web's adversity-hardened horse was long used to Dan'l, and had only acted up at first to be contrary, just like Web. The claybank took the bit easily now, even nuzzling Dan'l's shoulder for a moment.

"That's a good horse," Evan said, wiping his face to get the sleep out of his puffy eyes. It had only been a couple of hours rest, and his young body demanded more.

But Evan came to waking life with a grin as he added, "But I'd surely love to see Barry on your Lord Dunmore, Dan'l!"

Dan'l, too, laughed. "By God! That ugly roan will teach Barry quick who the master is."

"If they ain't all been put to the flames by now," Evan added, his mirth fading as he saddled his bay.

Dan'l scowled. "Boy, you got a sure way of killin' a funnin' mood."

The two set out through country that grew denser with trees as it neared the Missouri feeder known as French Lick. The Kentucky riders discovered the cache exactly where Dan'l had calculated they would. It was built into the side of a big hill, and had originally been constructed by French trappers to store plews and supplies. From the entrance it looked mighty knocked-together. But Dan'l had seen the insides of other such pelt-caches, and they were impressively secure and weather-tight.

Watching from a nearby covert, Dan'l and Evan soon verified that only two sentries—a Shawnee and a Fox, both with scalps tied to their clouts—guarded the entrance to the cache.

"No time for puttin' it to Parliament," Dan'l told Evan. "Can you hit vitals from here?"

Evan's mouth formed a grim, determined slit. He nodded. "You see what I see?"

Dan'l had indeed seen it, and something leaped inside him momentarily before he got control of it. But he had hoped Evan would not see it. Without doubt, the braided red hair dangling from the Shawnee's clout had once belonged to Tilly Hopewell, Evan's neighbor massacred at the mill with his family.

"I see it," Dan'l said. "Put it away from your thoughts, boy. You need to stay frosty if you mean to shoot plumb to lights at this range. We can't afford a miss. We'll shoot together on my command, y'unnerstan'?"

Evan swallowed audibly, but nodded. "Can I have the Shawnee?"

Dan'l nodded. He and Evan were already sprawled in prone positions. They dug out slight depressions to accommodate their aiming elbows. The Shawnee was chipping at an arrow point, now and then looking up to take a sweeping glance around. The smaller, heavier Fox brave sat on the ground near the entrance of the cache, his back to the hill as he smoked a clay pipe.

"Ready," Dan'l said, and both men brought their weapons up into firing position, locking the butts into their shoulder sockets.

"Take one deep breath," Dan'l said quietly, calming Evan, for it was a fairly long shot—perhaps two hundred yards or more. But they could not move closer without breaking cover.

"Let that air out slow and long and even," Dan'l went on. "Now let your whole body go heavy and relaxed, sink right in low. That's the gait, boy. Steady on. Now check your aim again since you've relaxed—there's the boy. Now take up the slack, son. Slow, just so sloww-w-w . . ."

Both long guns primer-popped, then bucked almost simultaneously. Dan'l's man was dead before his pipe shattered on the ground. Evan scored a good hit, but nonetheless, the Shawnee required a finishing shot to the head after the two men ran forward to check their enemies.

"No possum-players here," Dan'l certified. "Now turn away, Evan." Dan'l grabbed the obsidian knife from the beaded sheath of the Fox. "This won't be pretty, but there's no help for it if we mean to keep you alive until I burn that last cache."

Dan'l moved next to the dead Shawnee and steeled himself for the grisly task by recalling the scene at Blackford's Mill and the part this "brave" had played in it.

When he was finished with the knife, Dan'l tossed it aside and dragged the mutilated body to a tree out front of the cache. He propped it up and tied it into a sitting position with a short piece of rope around the neck.

"Merciful Jesus," Evan breathed when he risked a peek at it. "I understand why you put the Juju man around his neck. But why'd you carve out the Injun's eyes, Dan'l?"

"That ain't my natchral gait, boy. But we're over a barrel here. I ain't doing it to vent my spleen. These tribes believe that if your dead body is mutilated before it's washed and dressed for the Last Journey, then you spend eternity maimed that way. Ain't much they fear worse than to be blinded for eternity. We're warning 'em this is what waits for 'em inside, where you'll be holed up."

The cache, they quickly confirmed, had not been exaggerated in the reports: huge stores of pemmican and dried fruit; double-soled, knee-length elkskin moccasins preferred on the battle road for speed and stealth; oak war clubs, painstakingly fashioned by Indian artisans over many moons; buffalo-hair hackamores and ropes and reins; a huge pile of pine-shaft arrows; foxskin quivers; stone-tipped lances; tomahawks; a huge store of parched corn, good for men or ponies; and of course the kegs of nitre and sulfur to make gun-cotton.

"Well, you won't go hungry while you're waitin'," Dan'l remarked, stuffing some pemmican into his own parfleche. "C'mere, sprout."

Dan'l quickly showed the boy what to do when the time came—how to soak all the tow rags in the chemicals.

"Take a care when you spark it," Dan'l

warned. "Don't spill none of it on you. Remember . . . come sunup tomorrow, you be watchin' that northern and southern horizon. If the plan carries right, it should be mine that goes up first, then yours, then Web's. But if it comes down to the nut-cuttin' at Flat River, Web may torch his early—if he even got control of it. You see smoke clouds bilin' from either, let thissen rip, too. Then make a beeline back to the main group, if you can find 'em. Y'unnerstan'? Don't wait for me."

Evan nodded. His eyes slid to that dead Indian tied to the tree, his eyeless face staring down the slope at anyone foolish enough to come close.

"Don't worry, Dan'l. I'm hot to put at some redskins, I reckon. But I'll be damned glad to get shut of this place. *You* take a care, too. You got the hard part."

Dan'l worried once again about Web and the rest, busy as they must be trying to keep ahead of a foe that vastly outnumbered them.

" 'Pears to me," Dan'l replied, " 'hard parts' is the only kind we got. Includin' one by the name of War Hawk. So keep your powder dry, colt. The fandango ain't over yet."

Chapter Fifteen

Much later, in the twilight of his long life, Dan'l Boone would tell a historian: "I can't say as I was ever lost. I *was* bewildered once, though, for about three days."

And Dan'l came within a hair of being "bewildered" for a brief spell during the final ride to destroy the third cache. He rode through the night, sighting always on that distant headland, for it was said to contain the cache at its eastern end. But unexpected obstacles and dangers kept sending him into country where he lost his usual bearings.

The first serious delay came a few hours after he rode out from Flat River. Luckily, Dan'l was spelling the claybank at the time, leading it by the bridle around the shoulder of a low hill. The big explorer drew up short, his muscles tensing.

He had practically strolled through a spot near a seep spring where four Indian braves had camped!

Dan'l could count the buffalo-robe mounds around a still-smoldering fire. And farther back, four ponies had been tied to flexible tree branches, allowing them a little room to graze through the night.

Dan'l thanked the Good Lord he was cross-wind of the camp—neither the claybank nor the Indian mounts had yet whiffed each other and raised a ruckus. But it cankered at Dan'l that he couldn't account for this group's presence here. It must mean that War Hawk had *not* called all of his available braves to the Flat River area. These were most likely roving sentries, meaning they'd be on the prowl again by dawn. Dan'l prayed that Evan could hang on.

This discovery, and the dense pine forest to the east, left Dan'l no choice but to swing west around the camp. However, this move led Dan'l deeper into danger. He was leading the claybank out of a narrow defile when, abruptly, the horse reared up, eyes rolling back in baleful fear until the sockets were nearly all white.

Bear panic. The experienced long-hunter recognized it in an instant. Of all the things that a horse hated and feared, Dan'l reckoned bears and fires topped the list.

He led the claybank back into the defile and hobbled its forelegs.

"Sorry, old war horse," Dan'l muttered as he temporarily muzzled Web's horse with his sash.

"But I can't have you rousting out them Injuns behind us."

Dan'l crept forward to scout the situation, silently cursing yet another delay. It wasn't just Evan who was literally sitting in a death trap. Web and the rest, too, might be doing the same if the Obeah gimcracks and Juju dolls had worked. If not, Web's bunch were likely playing a lethal game of cat-and-mouse. And the cats could rest and eat while the mice wore themselves down running.

Dan'l crept out of the defile and paused to study the darkness. Ahead of him in a dimly lit clearing, a three-hundred-pound black bear rolled a log aside to get at the beetles under it. Dan'l knew black bears weren't nearly so vicious as brown bears or the ferocious silver-tips that some called grizzly bears. This one might even run if he shooed it off. Then again, it might attack. Bears were notional animals.

Dan'l cursed again. It was clear the bear, busy foraging, wasn't planning on going anywhere soon. Nor would Web's claybank go past it unless Dan'l swung even wider off course. There was naught else for it, Dan'l decided. When you can't dodge the bull, you take it by the horns. It that's true for the bull, he reasoned, why not the bear?

Dan'l rose up to his full height, filled his massive chest with air, and raised both brawny arms up to extend the impression of his already considerable size. Bears had keen smell and good hearing, but their eyesight was weak. All this one could see, Dan'l prayed, was a big, two-legged creature.

"Oooff-a!" Dan'l half-barked, half-coughed, imitating the noise of a grizzly asserting its territorial rights. *"Ooof!"*

The black bear spun round, sat back on its haunches to study him, and sniffed the air. When it suddenly dropped onto all fours, facing him, Dan'l's heart skipped a beat—should he try to kill it with his knife, or alert the sleeping Indians by firing his long gun?

But a moment later the bear snorted in fright and lumbered quickly off to the east, leaving this range to its superior relative. Dan'l returned for the claybank, and finally resumed his northward trek until he again spotted the huge, rising mass of the headland.

Exploring the end of the bluff in the cold predawn mist, Dan'l finally located the cache. It was built much like the last one, designed to take advantage of the bluff to hide everything except the narrow entrance. And this time, a nearly exhausted Dan'l discovered only one sentry, a Sauk. Clearly, War Hawk expected no trouble this far north.

Dan'l ground-hitched the claybank and crept closer to the spot where the sentry sat slumped near a cooking tripod. The day had lightened enough for Dan'l to make out a rawhide-and-horsehair bridle lying across the brave's knees. He had evidently been plaiting it when he fell asleep.

Dan'l started to sight in. But it chafed at him, this business of killing a man in his sleep. All his life Dan'l had spoken with contempt of the Spanish penchant for this practice. Now here he was, about to play the two-face.

Damn it all, he thought, lowering his rifle. Sure, he and Evan had flat out plugged those last sentries, bold as a turkey shoot. But those careless fools were awake, supposedly alert. If they let themselves be killed, it was their lookout, not Dan'l's. But *this* . . . it was mighty damned close to cold-blooded murder. Besides all that, Dan'l had no proof this red son had taken part in the Blackford's Mill massacre or any of the raids back east.

Then it occurred to Dan'l: He didn't have to kill this buck any more than he had to kill Barry Woodyard. Wit and wile could do Brother Ball's job. Dan'l could knock this buck on the head, tie him good, and just leave him for his people to free. *They* might kill him, but at least it would be off Dan'l's shoulders. The Boones had been called many things, but by God, "murderer" wasn't among them.

Moving from tree to rock to bush, Dan'l came in. Why, it's a bird's nest on the ground, he thought as the stuporous brave continued snoring.

Dan'l made sure the breechloader's mule-ear hammer was down. Then he swung his long gun in a fast arc, thwapping the sleeping brave just above the left ear.

Dan'l fully expected the Sauk to slump over, unconscious. Instead, the explorer cursed with surprise when the buck grabbed for the knife in his clout!

Damn my good intentions, Dan'l thought as he pinioned the brave's arms behind him. They struggled until the big man brought a crushing right knee into the Sauk's abdomen two or three times, taking the fight out of him.

"Hush that damn caterwaulin, John!" Dan'l growled as the Sauk began chanting his eerie, high-pitched death song. Dan'l used the name whites gave to all frontier Indians in direct address. "Ain't no white scalps on your sash, so yours won't dangle from mine."

Dan'l took the brave's knife and tied him securely to a pine tree out front. But when the big frontiersman turned to enter that cache, dizzying waves of exhaustion washed over him. No choice for it—despite the urgency, after he finished here, he and Web's claybank had to rest and eat.

Dan'l soon verified that this cache was similar to the last one. In jig time, Dan'l had turned plenty of tow cloth into volatile gun-cotton. From the entrance, he grabbed a smoldering stick from the sentry's fire and flipped it inside. The whooshing roar as the gun-cotton ignited sent a ball of heat rolling outward.

Soon, massive, dark black clouds of dense smoke belched out from the inferno within, rising straight up into the morning sky. Perhaps a quarter of an hour later, as a bleary-eyed Dan'l was searching out a place to bed down for a few hours, more black puffs of smoke appeared to the south.

Dan'l's face tugged into a triumphant grin. He was too far north to know yet if Web's bunch, too, had succeeded at Flat River. That was up to God Almighty. Dan'l Boone figured he had pulled *his* freight.

"Why, it was money for old rope!" Web Finley boasted. "This time, Boone, you had you a brainchild! W'an but a hour or so after you and Evan rode out that we found one of their pony herds. I killed a herd guard and rigged his body to his hoss. Put a shrunk head around his neck and them little devil dolls 'n' such all over his hoss. We sneaked him up to the bluffs and whumped his pony on the hinder."

"Laws, Colonel Boone!" Lonnie Papenhagen put in excitedly. "Them Injins seen that, and they lit out like hounds with their tails afire! They ain't showed up since."

"Soon's we seen Evan's cache smokin'," Corey chimed in, "we fired up our'n! Be a coon's age 'fore them redskins will be able to wage war on the eastern settlements again."

Sheltowee's Rangers, battle-weary and homesick, but also flushed with victory, had begun the long homeward journey. They were scattered now in pairs on the trace they'd hacked through the canebrakes on their way west. Evan, too, had made it back safely, and Dan'l knew he should feel the inner swelling of a solid and hard-won victory.

But Dan'l also knew it hadn't been a complete victory. Because War Hawk still lived. And so long as that mad dog roamed free, the massacre at Blackford's Mill went unavenged. And there was unfinished business for Sheltowee.

"Well, damn my eyes!" Web exclaimed.

He and Dan'l were riding vanguard. So they were the first to see it, blocking the trail ahead.

"The hell is that?" Steve Kitchens called out behind them. He stared, as did the rest, at the ornately carved pole someone had stuck in the ground. A piece of painted buckskin had been secured to the pole with rawhide thongs.

"Vengeance pole," Dan'l replied grimly. "War Hawk rode out and set it up. Them's his clan notches on the pole. He musta done it when he realized we foxed him with the Obeah."

"Then he's got to be mad as a badger in a barrel," Web said, "if he rode onto a white man's trace, one hemmed in like thissen."

Dan'l rode forward and tore loose the buckskin. It was covered with clay-paint pictographs. Web crowded close, and the two experienced trailsmen worked out the signs.

"That flock of red birds," Web said, "is the Indian nation."

"And the black bird that's flying alone," Dan'l said, "stands for War Hawk. He's sayin' he means to leave the tribe and 'fly alone.' And black means death to his enemies."

"That broke-in-two woman with the sun for her hair," Web continued in a quieter voice, "is Becky. And them little flowers busted off their stalks is your young'ns. He's tellin' you it don't matter that we stopped the war parties—we ain't stopped *him*. And he's making his brag that he means to come east alone and do for your family like he done for Evan's."

Dan'l nodded. "That's the way of it, all right."

All the men had crowded around him and Web, staring, waiting for Dan'l's reaction. Had they saved their own families at the price of his?

Dan'l took his time, meeting their eyes one by one: Web, Corey, Lonnie, Steve, Levy, all of them, even Stone Ludlow and Barry Woodyard. Yes, sure as death, Dan'l and War Hawk must someday meet. But Dan'l was damned if he would let the men's hard victory be tainted by this. War Hawk could issue all the threats he wanted to; Dan'l hadn't been born in the woods to be scared by an owl.

"You're all grit and a yard wide!" Dan'l roared out. "Alla you, tough as ary grizz!"

Dan'l swept his hat off and bowed from the waist in a salute to each and every one of his Rangers. He made a point of winking at Barry, and his former enemy winked back.

"Bastards all! Boone's bastards, and I'm proud to ride with you! When the next fight comes, we'll be ready for it. Now let's head home, you ugly sons of trouble!"

Every man joined in a lusty cheer for their colonel. Then, breaking into the rousing strains of "The Grenadier's March," the men from Kentucky rode east, toward the direction where bravery is born.

WHITE APACHE

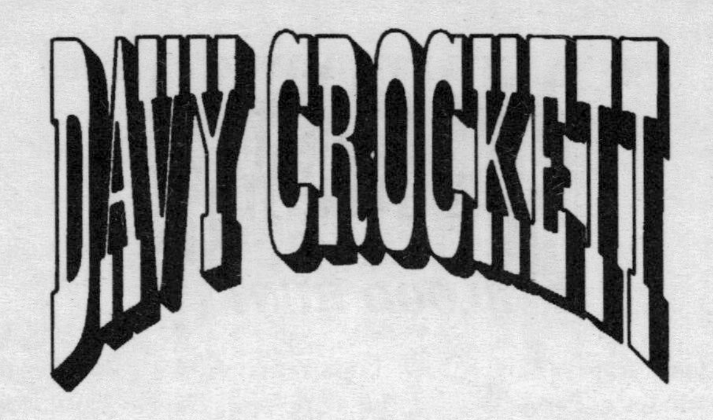
DAVY CROCKETT